Praise for Curt Leviant's Novels

T0051452

Nobel Laureate Saul Bellow on *The Yemenite Girl*
"I read straight through without a stop and with much interest. I enjoyed every turn of the story... *The Yemenite Girl* is done with great tact, feeling and skill."

Nobel Laureate Elie Wiesel on *The Man Who Thought He Was Messiah*
"This beautiful and moving fiction is the work of a gifted writer. Read it and plunge into an enchanting spiritual universe, filled with imagination, humor and warmth."

DIARY OF AN ADULTEROUS WOMAN -- a best-seller in Europe

"Astute character studies drive this sexy, witty, philosophically complex novel. Without sacrificing humor or character development, Leviant manages to write an ingenious romantic farce in the tradition of Vargas Llosa's Notebooks of Don Rigoberto."
Publishers Weekly

"Curt Leviant is a leading candidate for the title of best unknown American novelist. *Diary of an Adulterous Woman* is the novel that Tolstoy might have written instead of Anna Karenina had he been a modern American writer with an essentially comic sensibility. Compulsively readable and entertaining...The best novel I've read during the past ten years."
Chauncey Mabe, Book Editor, [Florida] *Sun-Sentinel*

"*Journal d'une femme adultere* — bright, funny and exciting -- is one of the surprise successes of the year... Curt Leviant is a supremely talented creative force [and his] art is brought to the highest level of incandescence."
Francois Busnel, *L'Express* (France)

"This novel is an immense story-telling machine... a modern *Decameron*."
Patrick Williams, *Elle* (France)

"A beautiful book that has been compared to *Madame Bovary, Anna Karenina* and *Lady Chatterley's Lover*, and whose author to Borges and Nabokov."
Il Venerdi Della Repubblica (Italy)

"A marvel. After having finished the book, you will begin all over again, reading the notes as well. Because the love story between Guido and Aviva is one of the most beautiful ever told."
Marieclaire (Italy)

"A modern *Decameron*, new and entertaining...They'll end up giving the Nobel Prize to Curt Leviant...who stealthily enters Spanish literature, almost in slippers, with his masterpiece. A sensational book."
Leer Magazine (Spain)

"*Diary of an Adulterous Woman* is one of the most impressive modern novels about love and seduction."

Capital Daily, Sofia (Bulgaria)

THE YEMENITE GIRL

"A passionate story… A true fiction… The tension between the charm of the text and the intensity of the subtext is what keeps the pages turning."

New York Times Book Review

"An imaginative novel…Beautiful touches of wit and poignancy."

Los Angeles Times

"A remarkable novel with excellent characterization, first-rate dialogue, and a love story with an unexpected ending. Contemporary – perhaps even immortal."

Philadelphia Bulletin

"The best novel I've had the luck to review this year and it may be the best novel many people will have the luck to read'"

Boston Globe

"Besides the plot and the romantic tangle, which gradually unravels, this novel is fascinating because, here, maybe for the first time, Israeli literature with its great voices becomes a myth … and all this thanks to a great American writer."

Elena Loewenthal, *La Stampa* (Italy)

"A small masterpiece by an author still little known in Italy."

Il Gazzettino (Italy)

THE MAN WHO THOUGHT HE WAS MESSIAH

"An enchanting, magical novel…sensual and intriguing…Exquisitely written, it will seduce and delight readers."

New York Times Book Review

"Spare, clean and poetic… Leviant's hypnotic fable is brilliantly wrought."

Publishers Weekly

"A novelist of awesome inventive talent…which makes him of the same lineage of Kafka, Saul Bellow and Agnon… A stunning novel."

Los Angeles Heritage

PARTITA IN VENICE

"A madcap adventure…magical telling…told with such infectious delight that it becomes a real joy to read."

Kirkus Reviews

"Witty and cleverly told…a gripping and whimsical tale."
Virginia Quarterly Review

"Curt Leviant's novel, Partita in Venice, is an irresistibly bright and erudite farcical comedy, written with the charm and caustic irony."

Florence Noiville, *Le Monde* (France)

LADIES AND GENTLEMEN,
THE ORIGINAL MUSIC OF THE HEBREW ALPHABET (two novellas):

"Not exactly Borges, not Kafka, not Calvino…but Curt Leviant's tales have the sounds, and music, of all three fabulists."
Alan Cheuse National Public Radio

"Leviant's solid craftsmanship and his Borgesian storytelling make this book an intriguing read."
Publishers Weekly

"Imagine a writer who combines the travel writing skills of Paul Theroux, the joy of language of Vladimir Nabokov, the inventive imagination of science fiction writer Stanislaw Lem and – voila – you have Curt Leviant, a writer who is fast on the heels of Saul Bellow."
Midstream Magazine

"Leviant is an original, wildly mystical, wildly comic, intensely Jewish, dazzling and inventive. I am in awe of the incredible richness of this book, its artistry, its grand design, its electric language."
Naamat Woman Magazine

"Two novellas about poetry and mystics and the nature of desire. The energy and passion of this desire flashes in Leviant's scintillating language and imagery."

Review of Contemporary Fiction

A NOVEL OF KLASS

"Reviewing each new book by Curt Leviant, I open with some variant of the same line: "Curt Leviant is the best unknown novelist in America." Ever since turning the last page my admiration for this novel has only grown. The hero, Ayzik Klass, is worthy of standing alongside of is Nick Carroway, Huck Finn, and Nathan Zuckerman, Sal Paradise. ONE OF THE TEN BEST BOOKS OF 2008."
Chauncey Mabe, Books Editor, *Sun-Sentinel*

"Some of Curt Leviant's previous novels have been compared to the works of foreign literary giants like Borges, Kafka and Calvino. His latest work, *A Novel of Klass*. suggests the influence of more domestic sources, including the Marx Brothers and S.J. Perelman. In his zany narrative – a comic story with two endings -- filled with brilliant satiric scenes, Leviant springs many surprises and offers a moving portrait of an exiled artist."

Leonard Fleischer, *The Forward.*

ZIX ZEXY ZTORIES

Listed in Paris's *Nouvelle Observateur* as:

One of the "TEN BEST BOOKS of 2015" published in France

"In France, he is known for his novel, *Journal d'une Femme Adultere (Diary of an Adulterous Woman)*, which, by its contents, just as by its cover, had driven men crazy. Curt Leviant goes at it again with *Zix Zexy Ztories*, six romantic fables that can be compared to Henry Miller's novels."

Didier Jacob, *Nouvelle Observateur* (France)

KING OF YIDDISH

"Beneath the linguistic panache and magical realism of Curt Leviant's infinitely readable *King of Yiddish* lie complex questions of family identity, vengeance and redemption. *King of Yiddish* is Leviant at his absurdist best."

Michelle Schingler, *Foreword*

"*King of Yiddish* is a page-turner, a comedic tour-de-force interspersed with a detective story."

Sidney Kessler, *New Jersey Jewish News*

KAFKA'S SON

"*Kafka's Son* is a work of genius."

France2 TV (Monique Atlan) [nationally telecast interview, March 2009

"Curt Leviant takes us along the trail of Kafka. Breathtaking!
As to whether or not Kafka had an heir — the answer is obvious. His name is Curt Leviant."

Andre Clavel, *LIRE Magazine* (France)

"Kafkaesque situations punctuate this quality novel which should establish Curt Leviant as a worthy heir of Franz Kafka himself."

Sandrine Szwarc, *Acutalite Juive* (France)

"The wizard Leviant recreates a mythical and fascinating Kafkaslovakia, in a wild baroque style. *Kafka's Son* is a thrilling novel."

Didier Jacob, *Nouvel Observateur* (France)

"Curt Leviant has written a great novel, pulsating with life and agitation."
Gerard-Georges, *Le Maire* (France)

"With the genius of a Salman Rushdie, Leviant grabs the reader's attention and keeps him in suspense until the final page."
Soundbeat Magazine (Canada)

"An enigmatic novel about identity and personal reinvention, *Kafka's Son* is both a moving tribute to Franz Kafka and a story of fate and miracles."
Michelle Schlinger, Jewish Book Council

Books by the Author

Fiction

Partita in Venice
A Novel of Klass
King of Yiddish
The Yeminite Girl
Kafka's Son
Katz or Cats: or, How Jesus Became My Rival in Love
Me, Mo, Mu, Ma, and Mod: Or, Which Will It Be, Me and Mazal, or
      Gila and Me
Diary of an Adulterous Woman: A Novel
Zix Zexy Ztories
Ladies & Gentlemen, the Original Music of the Hebrew Alphabet
      and *Weekend in Mustara* (two novellas)

TINOCCHIA
THE ADVENTURES OF
A JEWISH PUPPETTA

EDITED & TRANSLATED
From a Unique Manuscript

BY

Curt Leviant

with illustrations by
Nava Chefitz
Gracen Deerman
Laura Spero

Livingston Press

University of West Alabama

UWA
The UNIVERSITY of
WEST ALABAMA

Library of Congress Control Number: 2023939122
Printed on acid-free paper
Printed in the United States of America by
Publishers Graphics

Typesetting and page layout: Joe Taylor, Audrey Fondren
Proofreading: Annsley Johnsey, Angela Brooke Barger,
Savannah Beams,
Kaitlyn Clark, Tricia Taylor

Cover illustration and 'trees' (page 31): Leora Spero

Cover layout: Harry Chefitz

Frontispiece: Gracen Deering

All other illustrations: Nava Chefitz

Acknowledgement:

I would like to thank the Siena native, Professor Gioacchino Durante, formerly the Salvatore and Sofia Umbriago Professor of Italian Language, Literature and Culture at Columbia University, for helping me with the Sienese localisms scattered throughout the manuscript.

C.L.

6 5 4 3 2 1

TINOCCHIA
THE ADVENTURES OF
A JEWISH PUPPETTA

This book is dedicated to
Harry Chefitz,
my son-in-law,
with thanks for his
artistic graphic cover design,
and to his two daughters,
my grand-daughters,
Leora Spero
for her attractive cover art work
and lovely illustration
and
Nava Chefitz
for her superb illustrations.

All three have captured
the playful spirit of Tinocchia
with verve and imagination.

Editor's Introduction

It began like this.

I was doing research in the old Municipal Library in Siena on the history of the local Jewish community, looking at a couple of hand-written Hebrew memoirs of life in Siena in the early 1800's. I sat all alone – and that was one of the marvels of working in this quiet, almost forgotten library – at the long, polished oak table in the small, intimate archives room, on the third floor, with its attic-sloped ceiling, where the shelves on one wall were filled with what looked like old, wide shoe boxes.

Getting up to stretch my legs, to take a break from the tightly calligraphed Hebrew manuscripts I was reading, I walked around the table and began looking at the boxes.

All were labeled on the narrow side of the lid. Only one was not. Unusual configurations always spark my curiosity. Why is this box not labelled? I wondered. And so I pulled out the dusty box and saw writing on the long side of the lid. The letters were very small but I was able to make out the old-fashioned Italian script, in mid- to late-nineteenth century ligatures, long, elegant and slightly slanted. I read the word: "Tinocchia."

That word's proximity to the name of the famous long-nosed puppet fascinated me. The two names had the same number of letters, were spelled the same way, and had almost the same pro-nunciation. Only the initial "T" and the final "a" were different. Also, there seemed to be a Hebrew word imbedded in the name. Was this accidental, or did the author know some Hebrew?

The box was wrapped neatly, even professionally, with beige brown string. In the way it was tied, one could see the hand of old European shopkeepers who with esthetics and skill knew how to make a package both attractive and secure. One could almost sense the final flourish of the fingers on the little bow on top.

When I lifted the dusty box – I didn't blow the dust away and make a face as you read in storybooks, but wiped it away carefully with a couple of tissues in my pocket – I saw the name Carlo Lorenzini written with pencil on top of the lid. I repeated the name in my mind. Sounded familiar. From where do I know that name? It flickered for a moment on the tip of my consciousness. Recognition almost surfaced, then faded. But a moment later – bam! It came to me. Lorenzini. The real name of Carlo Collodi, the author's nom de plume.

Oh, my God, I whispered, intrigued and excited. Collodi, the author of *Pinocchio*.

Suddenly, I felt a surge, like an electric jolt! And when I calmed down I noticed what was most fascinating: there was a little question mark after the name Lorenzini, as though the archivist, or whoever handled this box, was obliged to record his doubt. Suddenly, words that had not been aligned fell into formation.

Tinocchia – Collodi.

Could this really be? This box was probably misfiled by the librarian who didn't connect Lorenzini with Collodi.

If indeed this box contained something by Collodi, was it some Jewish joke the noted nineteenth century Italian author was playing? Or had someone who knew Hebrew helped him?

I put my finger on the tight thin string. It vibrated under my touch like a string on an old violin. Don't think I didn't hesitate, as I considered that old twisted string with the exquisite bow knot. What had this box to do with my research? Should I ask for permission to examine this box? I looked to my left to the door. But then I put all concerns, hesitations and qualms aside. The librarian who guided me upstairs to this room did not tell me that anything here was off limits. I was in a library. Once permission was granted to have access to the stacks a researcher could look at anything. And so I decided to undo that beautifully tied knot.

Without excessively romanticizing it, I was doing, rather undoing, what was destined: answering the magnetic pull of an unopened string on a dusty old box with the name Lorenzini written on it in an ornate, neatly scripted hand.

If this box indeed contained a manuscript written by Collodi, then the title confirmed what I had suspected. And as my imagination heated up, I fantasized that perhaps the old master of *Pinocchio* had written – if the label atop the box was correct, and the question mark deleted – a book about a girl puppet, or puppetta, with the Hebrew/ Italian name of Tinocchia. What an ingenious pun!

On the first page, in clear Italian, the author writes that this manuscript was given to him by Abramo Livorno, the beadle of the Siena synagogue. Well, then I'm in home territory, ran the thought through my mind; it fits right into the research I'm doing on Siena; a find of the first order!

And then, in a new paragraph below that line, Lorenzini/ Collodi, or whoever wrote the manuscript, dedicates the book to his friend, the same Abramo Livorno, who had helped him with Jewish matter in the book and even gave him some ideas.

But here was a problem. A couple of days later, when I checked in the archives of the Siena synagogue, which lists all the rabbis and all the beadles from the early 17th century through the mid-twentieth century, and the years they served, I could not find an Abramo Livorno. Was it possible that he was not listed? Or was there some other reason for omitting his name?

Since this manuscript was more than one hundred twenty years old, likely written after the serialized publication of *Pinocchio* in 1881, any copyright would have expired. In any case, no copy- right could exist, since as far as I know only a published book can be copyrighted.

So I photographed the mss with my phone, page by page.

And I didn't feel too bad doing this. The latter phrase needs explanation and elaboration. Indeed, I felt some qualms because I took something (even though I removed, that is, took, nothing) from a library without permission. But, on the other hand, I knew that sooner or later (more likely, later) permission would have been given, after much bureaucratic delay, filled out forms, official rubber stamps, many signatures, and, finally, impressive, old-fashioned scarlet wax seals.

My view is that this imaginative work, with its affinity to Collodi's classic, after being lost or forgotten or misfiled or misplaced for more than a century, should be brought to light sooner rather than later.

What is remarkable too is that this found manuscript contains a complete, or almost complete, and perfectly preserved, old Italian Purim-shpil in rhymed verse, which the anonymous author transcribed and inserted into his fantasy. I consulted with a couple of rabbis from north and central Italy and none knew of any extant Purim-shpils. The tradition for presenting a humorous play on Purim night based on the story in the biblical Book of Esther was not as well-rooted in Italy as it was in Eastern Europe, although the Carnivale in Italy may have had some influence on it. The author may have created this rhymed Purim play, based on something he remembered from childhood, or he may have had an actual manuscript and inserted it. Another possibility is a combination of all of the above.

(I remember one summer evening during the Carnivale in Venice, passersby hurling extemporized lines of verse at one another in a melodic chant that I imagine was very much like the sing-song of the Purim-shpil.)

I should add that each day when I left the library the guard politely, and with a mien of regret, and even apologizing, shyly inspected my briefcase; it didn't dawn on him to look at my phone.

When I returned to the United States, I showed this manuscript (reproduced and enlarged from the images on my phone) to two Italian specialists in late 19th century Italian literature; neither could conclusively identify the author. These two learned men wanted to remain anonymous, but they permitted me to summarize their views. One said that if indeed Collodi is the author, he certainly knew a lot about the Jewish tradition or got lots of help from someone who knew it. And if it is Collodi he occasionally pokes fun at himself in a clever manner, which you will soon see for yourself. The other professor tended to believe that an anonymous Jewish writer composed this thoroughly Jewish book; only a Jew would know so many details about Jewish life, customs, and holidays. And this second professor also feels that it is a Jew writing a book similar to Collodi's, in tribute to the author of *Pinocchio*.

Taking the latter's view into consideration, a new light now shines on the entire Abramo Livorno episode and helps explain his omission from the Siena synagogue archives. The scenario of a gift of the mss by Livorno to the anonymous author and his subsequent dedication of the book to him might very well be a hoax, very typical of 18th and 19th century English literature, where either the hoax or the "found" manuscript was popular. The most famous of these, of course, are *Gulliver's Travels* and *Robinson Crusoe*. But whatever the truth is, it is hidden from us now, and what remains is this magnificently imagined "colleague" to the Pinocchio story, now cast with a feminine hero and in a Jewish slant.

For some unknown reason this book was never submitted for publication and librarians of a bygone era packed the pages into a box, perhaps mistakenly labeled Lorenzini (with a face-saving question mark), and it lay untouched here in the dusty archives room on the third floor of the Siena Municipal Library until curious fingers (re) discovered it.

As I began to re-read the manuscript, I leaned toward the first professor's view that Collodi himself composed this "sequel" with help from a Jewish friend. But the more I read the more I was persuaded that, given the detailed and accurate Jewish content of some scenes, the second professor was very likely right, although we have no definitive proof.

If a reader asks, How do you know it's not by Collodi, I respond how could Collodi know so much of Jewish matter? On the other hand, if it *is* by Collodi, why would he make fun of himself by putting in Pinocchio's mouth criticism of his own tendentious "go to school" advice, which he keeps repeating in *Pinocchio*, supplanting the esthetics of story with preaching?

If this mss is indeed by the author of *Pinocchio*, he certainly mastered the inner traditions of the Jewish holiday of Purim. Could he have been coached by a Jewish friend in town? The impossible-to-find synagogue sexton, Abramo Livorno? In fact, could the latter have composed the Purim-shpil? I indicated a possible hoax above, but such are the vagaries of thoughts and suppositions when one has little to go on.

And so, I believe it is best to assume, unless further research and serendipitous discovery proves otherwise, that *Tinocchia* is an anonymous work. The truth is, in the absence of verifiable evidence, we will never know who wrote the following pages.

As far as I can tell we have before us the complete story. However, there are two or three instances in the book where the author left in two differing versions of a fact or an adventure, unsure of which one to include. He had evidently hoped to return to the manuscript and make the correction. Obviously, for some reason, he did not do so, and so for those pages I make an editorial comment to draw the reader's attention to both versions.

It's worth noting that I was so taken by this engaging mss and its lively adventures that I postponed my Siena project and undertook to translate this book, to present it to the reading public.

And now, I, who am only the finder, translator, and editor of this marvelous handwritten Italian manuscript, will withdraw into the woodwork, and let the puppetta herself tell the story in her own words, the very words I discovered on that marvelous day in the archives room of the Siena Municipal Library, not one word altered, not one letter changed, and rendered faithfully and to the best of my ability, from the late 19th century Tuscan Italian, into English.

C. L.

Everything is possible in an impossible world.

T.

1

Once upon a time there was a puppetta.

What's a puppetta?

Definition coming.

And what's its name?

Read on, dear reader, read on, and soon you will know.

Maybe even sooner than that.

My name is Tinocchia.

You notice I don't begin this true narrative, this memoir, by opening with the words, "Call me Tinocchia," in imitation of that popular American novel about a great whale. But if you like whales, before long you will meet a great fish.

Tinocchia has a familiar ring, doesn't it? I'm a puppetta, that is, a girl puppet (a boy puppet, he's a puppetto). Yes, Tinocchia *is* a rather strange name, I know, so un-Italian. No other girl in Italy has it, but you must agree that it has a thoroughly Italian sound.

You see, my name is a clever Hebrew concoction thought up by my Papa. Everyone calls him Giuseppe, but I call him by his Hebrew name, Yossi.

Yossi's good friend, Geppetto, was also a woodworker like my Papa. Some years ago he created a puppet, actually a mario-nette, to whom he gave a name – well, I don't have to tell you, for everyone, as the famous puppetto himself would cleverly say, it's a name that everyone knose.* Soon thereafter Geppetto invited Yossi to come take a look.

This inspired Papa to make a puppetto too.

Me.

To name me. Papa Yossi played with the Hebrew word for "baby", *tinok*, and with a nod to his friend's creation, he called me Ti-nocchia. Much later he would tell me many more fascinating details about my name and its links to the Hebrew alphabet, and even to the opening words of the Torah.

--- --- --- --- --- --- --- --- --- --- --- --- --- --- --- --- --- --- --- ---

*In the original, "*conaso*," a pun conflation of the two Italian words, *conosce* (knows) and *naso* (nose). If *conaso* is separated into two words – *con naso* – it can also mean "with nose." My rendition, "knose," is but a pale attempt at recreating the anonymous author's brilliant Italian word play.

2
Yossi's Litvish Background
and Why His Grandfather Moved to Italy

Let me give you some background on my Papa Yossi. Yossi's grandfather, my great-grandfather, left Vilna, Lithuania during the height of the fame of the Vilna Gaon, around the 1760's, more than one hundred years ago, and settled in central Italy to find religious freedom. He found it among the tolerant Italian Jews in Siena. Even though he was an Ashkenazic Jew—since he came from Lithuania, he was called Litvish—he was accepted by his fellow Italian Jews, some of whom traced their ancestry in Italy back for hundreds of years.

What prompted Yossi's grandfather to leave Vilna? He didn't like the idea of Jews burning the books of other Jews. He thought this was sacrilege, a desecration of God's name. Jews write books. Jews print books. Jews don't burn books. And when the Vilna Gaon, the most respected and famous Jew in Vilna in the late 18th century, began burning the books written by the Hasidim, whom he despised, Yossi's grandfather – although he wasn't a Hasid – decided to pluck up his roots and move elsewhere.

He found refuge and welcome in Siena.

And his grandson, my Papa Yossi, Giuseppe to his Italian friends, lived happily in Siena, where he made his living as a first-class woodworker. Yossi was bright, practical, wise. He got a good education in Italian and in Hebrew, and he passed this knowledge on to me.

Yossi was solidly built, a good-looking man with a fleshy nose. At about, 5'8" he was taller than most of the men in the neighborhood. He had almost no hair except on the side of his head and by his sideburns. But it was lush black; not a thread of white in it. Yossi always had a pleasant demeanor. As soon as anyone spoke to him, a smile lit up his open, round face, and at once came a little welcoming gesture: raised eyebrows and a warm light in his eyes greeted the person he was facing. He called this the sparks of day-light that he said was in all of us. This light-filled smile is what most people remember him by – that from-the-heart genial demeanor.

And the demeanor was the man. His kind nature was reflect-ed in his deeds. When he heard of a poor family that had a small fire in their house that destroyed some of their cabinets, Yossi built new ones for them, as his gift. When the synagogue had appeals for money to help the poor, Yossi always gave generously, and not only to Jews, but to non-Jews as well. From his example I learned too.

3
Tinocchia Discussing Her Origins and Learning How to Speak

Although I speak now, I should say that after Yossi fashioned me I couldn't at first. I could hear and understand but I could not speak because no one spoke to me. I heard him talking all the time but he never addressed his remarks to me. He hadn't realized I was capable of speaking. It just didn't dawn on him that I could. I don't know what made him do it, but one day, as I was sitting in a chair, he came up to me and said:

"Tinocchia, you were born into Italian. You hear it all around you. But I also want you to know Hebrew, so I will begin to teach you Hebrew. You will be able to read and understand. Yes?"

"Yes."

He backed away. I could see the astonishment on his face. But then he continued:

"You said, Yes?"

"Yes," I said again.

"Can you say more than Yes?"

"Yes."

"Hmm, but that's still the same word. Who taught you?"

"You."

"Can you say more than Yes and You?"

I laughed. "Yes."

And Papa laughed too.

Then I said:

"Yes. You. Begin. Hebrew. By speaking to me you're teaching me. Now that you're talking to me, all the words I've heard you say to other people, now they can come out of me."

"How unusual. Astonishing. Even miraculous. You're a talking golem."

"What's a golem, Papa?"

"That's something like a marionette, except it's made out

of clay and not out of wood. And a golem can't talk. He just follows orders and can't think very much. And now you, Tinocchia, talking! This is miraculous. A talking marionette, or puppetto, like the one my woodworker friend, Geppetto, made. And I had thought that only he could make one speak. So from now on you too will be speaking and learning Hebrew in addition to Italian."

At that time I had not yet met his woodworker friend's pup-petto. But I would get to meet him soon enough. And it was by – and because of – an accident.

4
She Loves the Smell of Wood

I love the smell of wood. For me it is like breathing fresh air in the forest. It is amazing, my first sensation, that open, slightly moist aroma of freshly planed pine; or, the rose of roses, the rare red mahogany, with its perfume like dusky wine, or the elegant teak with the exotic scent, tinged with spices, released as Yossi's saw cuts through. But pine is the most plentiful and it is its fragrance that surrounds you like a hug, and I can inhale it – even in memory – even when I am far away from the workshop. Isn't that strange, to be able to remember an aroma? As I breathe in, along with the air that rushes past my nostrils, I smell that unique, pungent, sweet smell of cut pine.

Which I am made of.

5
Yossi Shows Tinocchia Trees in the Woods

When I was a little girl, I asked my father, "Where do puppettos come from? How are they made?"

Papa Yossi replied: "I will answer like a good woodworker: they come from where all good things – and some bad – come from: the outdoors. The woods. The forest. Come with me. It's a beautiful sunny day. It's a good time to show you."

I followed Yossi out the back door of the house, across the small meadow, to where the woods began. The scent of the trees and the leaves and dried pine needles on the ground, oh, all of that was so delicious. Like the rarest perfume. He approached a shiny dark pine tree, tapped it tenderly; he touched, he almost held it in embrace.

"From this type of tree comes almost everything I make. It's mine and Geppetto's favorite: the carpentree."

Then he said:

"And here, this one, look. This is a very special, magical pine, the finest, most sensitive wood. That's where you and Pinocchio come from. It's called the puppetree... Look around, Tinocchia, see, all kinds of trees grow in this wonderful forest. You've never been here before, right?"

"Yes, Papa. You told me not to go into the woods by myself."

Papa Yossi walked deeper into the woods with me, along a little path strewn with dried beige and light brown pine needles. In a little clearing stood two beautiful trees with orange golden leaves, the sort you see in late October. But it was still spring.

"These two trees are associated with creative people. This one gives us easels and frames and paint brushes. It's the artistree. And from this one, writing desks and bookshelves, and paper and pencils too. This is the poetree."

Then Papa put his index finger on an oddly shaped little

brown tree, which looked like a little pole.

"Here chickens grow. Guess its name."

"Papa, you must be joking. Chickens don't grow on trees."

"Try to name it," he said, trying to suppress a twinkle in his eye.

"Fricasee?"

"No. It's the poultree."

But I'm sure he was joking. There was nothing on that tree that even gave the hint of a hen.

Now we walked deeper into the forest; the light was thinner. The sunlight barely filtered through the high dark oaks. In a little clearing three trees stood by themselves.

"Of these trees," Yossi said softly, seemingly in awe of them, "you don't want the fruit. An example of what I said before. Because some bad things also come from the forest, like poison mushrooms. Trees are like people, some good, some bad. See this tree, with leaves like happy-faced sun gods? This is the idolatree. And this one, with the swinging branches and seductive fruit, is the harlot-ree. And this bigger one with tight, angry branches and close-lipped leaves – this one is the bigotree."

"And where do real babies come from, Papa? Do they also come from here?"

"Of course, I'll show you. It's the most beautiful tree of all, with slender trunk and, ah, here it is, see its graceful, chartreuse leaves, and rose-tinged milk white blossoms? Isn't it pretty?"

"It is, Papa. What's it called?"

"This one is the infantree."

Then I pointed to another tree, different from the others. It seemed to have a certain appeal and yet I could sense there was a question mark about it. "And that one?"

"Oh, that one? It has a strange name, that tree. All lands and all nations have it as its source. All men pledge allegiance to it and fight for the right to possess it and dwell in it. In England and in America they even have a song for it. 'My Countree'."

"How about that one, with the odd-shaped leaves like unusual letters or numbers."

"Ah, yes. That's the plane geometree, which helps us woodworkers keep straight lines."

After I thanked Papa Yossi for this little excursion in the woods he said:

"When you'll be a little older and are able to understand, I will tell you some fascinating things about yourself and your unusual name."

6
Fear of Fire. Blowing Out the Hanukkah Lights

But I must admit there are problems. Sometimes it's no fun being made of wood. Especially during Hanukkah. I have an inborn fear of fire. If you're made of wood you have to have a thousand eyes. Fear of fire always shadows you. You don't stay in a room with a fireplace; being in a room with a wood-burning stove makes me shiver. You take a detour around people who smoke on the street.

Consider this: imagine you're an ice sculpture and you're put out into a sunny garden noontime in July.

When Papa Yossi lit the Hanukkah oil lamp, I moved to the back of the room. Once, when I was about five or six, when he left the room, so afraid was I of fire, I blew the flames out. It was the second night of the holiday. Yossi too was afraid of fire and made no secret of it, for in his workshop, with wood all over the place, there was always a danger. That is why, just in case, he kept jugs of water scattered in various places in the workshop.

You should have seen the look on his face when he came back into the room and saw the tiny dry black wicks.

"Oh, my," he said. "The wind must have blown them out. But there are no open windows here. So how could this happen?"

"It's me," I said. "I did it."

"Well, at least you're honest."

But I didn't know what that word meant. I had not heard it before.

"Why did you do this, Tinocchia?"

"I was afraid, Papa, afraid of the flames. The live fire makes me nervous... Although fire is hot, even looking at it sends cold shivers through me."

"But one should not blow out the lights over which a blessing has been recited. Not Hanukkah lights, not Shabbat lights, not holiday lights."

Still, Papa looked at me sympathetically; he was not angry, for he said as he relit the oil lamp:

"I too would not leave a fire unattended. But I knew you were here. From now on I will stay in the room with you until the Hanukkah lights burn down."

7
Tinocchia Marveling at Letters and Reading

I loved to read. Most of all adventures. And every time I read one, especially if the heroine was a girl like me, I felt that adventure. I actually sensed that it was me traveling through space and landing in Peru or in the frozen north of Norway, and I longed to go on such an adventure of my own. Just like the fictional heroes I read about had succeeded, I would succeed too.

I also remember reading that time cannot be measured in days the way money is measured in lire, because while all lire are equal, every day, perhaps even every hour, is different.

Whoever said that was absolutely right, for some days are longer than others. Some go quick as an eyeblink – with others you slog through tar. Time is not in our clocks; it's in our heads. An old man, ill, bored, sits in his chair and the minutes tick slowly tock like hours. Yet when I immerse myself in a favorite book the hours rush by like a rain-driven stream.

Before I learned to read it always amazed me that someone could make some signs on a piece of paper and everyone could understand them and agreed what it meant. It wasn't a private scribble. And via post you could send these signs on paper to a friend in another town who would understand the thoughts in your head. Even when I learned to read and write, I still marveled at those signs like "m" and "p", or the sound made by letters that spell "tin." What a wonderful invention was the alphabet. All I had to do was shape the letters properly and I could speak to someone far away without even making a sound.

And the same held true for the Hebrew alphabet, but this time from right to left. I was so proud that Papa Yossi gave me the opportunity to learn another alphabet.

I also wondered about the magic we speak into the air. We don't see these invisible letters of the words but yet people understand us. And if those words are chanted or sung we remember them even better. It's always easier to remember words if music is linked to them. Later, when I was in a difficult situation – it was actually my first real live adventure – it was a melody, a Purim melody, that helped me.

Listen to what I experienced one day.

I saw the words I was saying. They hovered out there, in space, neatly spelled out. They were a kind of silent echo to what I had just uttered. But since it only happened two or three times, I didn't tell Yossi. And the words remained in the air just the way I said them, as if on a transparent placard; and then, after a while, they too vanished. The only way to make words really stay is to write them down. That's the way they last. Until you throw that piece of paper away.

In the synagogue another marvel, with words from the Siddur, the prayer book. When I went to services on Sabbaths or holidays with my Papa Yossi and we sang the melodies along with the rest of the congregation, I felt the Hebrew letters dancing on my palms. I would put down my Siddur, hold my palms on my lap face up, and see the dance of the letters in the shape of words. This lasted only as long as the melody was sung. Once the song was over the letters disappeared.

And one more sensation, this one very personal, when I recited the Hebrew blessing thanking God for fruit, *boh-reh p'ree ha-etz*, "who creates the fruit of the tree." At the word *etz*, "tree," a wave, a thrill, a sympathetic vibration – it felt like an inner light or glow, yes, one of Yossi's sparks – would circle through all my limbs.

8
Try-outs for Purim-shpil Announced in Shul

I looked at the Jewish calendar. It was March. The holiday of Purim was approaching. And sure enough, the next Saturday, at the end of the Shabbat morning services in the Siena synagogue, Rabbino Davide dei Rossi told the congregation that Papa has an important announcement to share about the traditional Purim-shpil.

Yossi stood and said that the try-outs for parts in the humorous, rhymed play would start the following week, on Thursday evening, at 7 pm, in the downstairs social hall. He also said he had already notified the non-Jews who had participated or had come in previous years about the auditions.

Yes, my Papa Yossi had initiated this custom of presenting a Purim-shpil years ago and it had been a great success.

He also told me that this year I was big enough to try out for a part, either a major role or to be a member of the chorus.

"I'd like to be Esther."

"Fine. But why?"

"I had a dream last night that I was in a folktale and I was the good queen. So now I want to be a real live make-believe queen."

"So come to the audition," Papa Yossi said, "and try out for the part. But first you have to re-read the story."

I opened the Bible and read the Book of Esther, which is called a "megillah," since it's written like a scroll. Now I had no doubt that I wanted the role of Queen Esther.

I thought that the try-outs would be a great adventure, but before the Purim-shpil auditions I had a real adventure and quite a scary one too.

We'll get to that soon enough. First I want to tell you about somebody I bumped into whom I had heard about but didn't know.

9
A Downhill Ride and Bumping Into ...

As I was going out for a walk I heard a tiny voice: "Don't forget about me."

"What did you say, Tinocchia?" Papa asked me.

"I didn't say a word."

"Then who spoke just now?"

"It's me," came the little voice again. "How come you, Tinocchia, a piece of wood like me, can talk and jump and run, but me, I'm also made of wood, am stuck here on the floor? Why should I be glued here in the corner all the time?"

I looked closely. It was the little table talking, the one Yossi had made for me. Not the big old scarred oaken table in the dining room but the small one that stood next to the wall where I put some of my books. His speaking gave me an idea. In his workshop Papa had some roller wheels, just like the ones kids have on their skates. So I asked Papa to put four rollers on the little table's four legs.

Now I had a little cart of my own. And there was a little box with tiny walls on all four sides for me to sit. The fascinating part, though, was that this little table seemed to have a soul of its own. For when I called out to Papa in the workshop that I'm going to take the table for a ride, it rode over to me on its own from the corner where it stood.

"All right," I said, "since you're so clever, you're also going to have a name – Table."

"Not terribly imaginative," he muttered, "but it's better than Giacomo."

As we rolled downhill, he sang out, "Whee!" and I saw a boy wearing a white cap trying to cross the street without looking. I couldn't stop in time and Table grazed his heel. The boy gave out a muffled cry of pain, then leaped up – I saw his cap falling – and caught hold of a low birch branch overhanging the street and began swinging.

I saw he was a puppetto like me. I stopped and apologized.

"I'm so sorry. I couldn't stop in time. You rushed into the street so quickly."

The boy dropped down from the tree, dusted himself off, and stood opposite me on the sidewalk. He picked up his white cap, blew at it, slapped it on his thigh several times, then put it back on his head. He was a bit older than me and somewhat taller. He had a perky face and a cute, longish, pointy nose.

Neither of us said, "Why don't you watch where you're going?"

The puppetto stared at me. Perhaps he was mute.

"Can you talk?" I asked carefully, politely.

"Yes."

"Can you say more than Yes?"

And I laughed, remembering Papa Yossi's first conversation with me.

"Yes," the puppetto said and then he said no more.

"So why the silence?"

"I didn't think you could talk."

"But didn't you hear me apologize to you?"

"No. I can talk but I can't hear."

We both laughed.

I had expected his voice to be as pointy as his nose but it wasn't; it had a smooth, pleasant tone.

We stood there for a moment, each taking in the other. Even though he was a puppetto, and even though there were many things we could have said to each other like, who made you, and where do you live, we said nothing. I just looked at him again for a moment and then continued on my way, rolling with Table even further down the hill.

I didn't even ask him his name.

At the end of the ride Table said: "That's more like it. Now I feel I'm part of the world. No more heavy loads on my chest."

Now I will record the scary adventure I was hinting at earlier.

10
A Visitor

One evening in my room – in Italian this phrase sounds so banal, all five words* ending in the feminine 'a'; yet these simple five words, each with a repetitive, rhythmic two syllables – one evening in my room – may cloak the stirring, stunning, shattering event that was about to take place.

One evening in my room I heard a voice. It was 7:15 by the clock on my dark green chest of drawers that Papa Yossi had made for me, and shreds of daylight still were scattered in the blue spring sky. I should have been scared – a voice from nowhere – but I wasn't. In fact, I was unusually calm.

First the voice, then the person. He stood there, a rather tall man, probably in his mid-fifties, with a thin grey mustache, wearing a dark blue suit and a not very memorable tie. Unlike such characters in children's books, he wasn't wearing a long black cloak and he didn't look ominous.

"Who are you?" I asked at once, "and what are you doing here?"

"I am called Sam."

"Sam who?"

"You're not pronouncing it right. It's not Sem, like in the word 'memoria'. My name has the long 'aaah', like in 'bambino'. Saaahm."

"Wait a minute. *Sam* means 'poison' in Hebrew."

"I see you know the holy tongue. But Sam is just the short form of my name."

Now I was scared. My voice quaked as I asked, "What's your full name?" even though I knew full well what he would say.

"Samael."

El, God's name, was linked to his basic name: venom.

--- --- --- --- --- --- --- --- --- --- --- --- --- --- --- --- --- ---

*In the original: *una sera nella mia stanza*.

"But that means you're the Angel of...the Black Angel."

"I'm in the habit of speaking directly. So I will say, Yes."

I felt the walls of the room coming closer. Had he come for me?

"Yes," Samael said again, as if reading my mind. "Erase the as if."

Without moving, the walls drew near. Any closer I would not breathe.

I wanted to ask out loud but was afraid to. For he had already said Yes to my unasked question.

When walls approach one looks for exit. So I said:

"How do I know it's not someone else's voice talking to me, using the Tetragrammaton?"

At the mention of God's holy four-letter Hebrew name, Samael seemed thrust back a step. I wished I had the power of the ancient sages of the Midrash to confront the Dark Angel with God's awesome name. To stretch out my hand, index finger out, utter God's holy name, and make him disappear.

Samael's answer was a pointed silence.

At that moment I noticed two things: he had not once addressed me by my name; and it was only then, during that still moment, that I first saw the long scabbard on his left side.

"You know why I am here."

Should I play the innocent and make believe I did not know? But if I said Yes wouldn't I be following a script I didn't want to follow?

I did not reply. Like Samael I could be silent too.

The Dark Angel looked at me. I had never before seen such an unfeeling, impassive look on a person's face.

And then, I don't know where it came from, or why, a sudden surge of courage rose in me, an elixir that spread through all my limbs.

"What? You've come for me?" Soon as I heard my voice the room's space expanded. I felt I could breathe again. "It's not fair. I'm young. I've just begun to write my story."

"We don't live in a storybook world. Young, old. Good, bad. It doesn't matter."

"What did I do wrong that you've come for me?"

"Nothing."

"Then where is justice?"

Samael gave out crisp, sarcastic laugh.

"Fairness and justice do not concern me. I am exempt from justice. In this matter it is pure chance. Some get it early, some get it late. There is no justice. It's just plain fate."

I could not miss the rhyme of his last remarks. Was this too pure chance, or was he just a nasty Purim-shpiller in disguise.

But I couldn't – didn't want to – stop talking. At that moment I felt the who of who I was. My soul, rich and light, full as the rising sun, and the sparks of Yossi's daylight vibrant in me. I felt mighty. I sensed I could do battle with Samael.

I watched his right hand. It did not move to his left side. It made no move at all in that direction.

"Whoever heard of a heroine of a book..." and now I didn't hesitate to use the word, "dying in the beginning of a story?" I had heard what he said about fairness but I couldn't help repeating, "It's not fair."

"I told you fairness does not concern me. Nor beginnings. Just endings," he said drily. "And books are not my concern either."

I noticed too that unlike the Talmudic maxim that one should answer in order, first first, last last, Samael did just the reverse. He answered my last point first and my first point last.

"Then what is your concern?"

"Life. The real world.... I have a mission. Everyone of woman born is destined to meet with me."

Hearing this I jumped; my body literally jerked. I felt relief. As though I'd been spared torment. Had Samael understood the words he had just uttered?

"But I am not of woman born," I shouted, happy. I proclaimed it as if it was the final sting in a debate. No counter-argument to a riposte like that. "I am a puppetta. Made of pine by Giuseppe, my Papa Yossi, the woodworker."

I thought Samael would think this over and make some weak reply, but he said at once:

"But since you live and speak and act like a human being you are included too."

What could I say to that? His words surprised me. But what he said next surprised me even more.

"I am permitted to tell you...you will go straight to puppetta heaven."

I had no interest in that. That did not attract me at all.

"I'd rather stay here and continue my work."

The Dark Angel shook his head. He did not say a word, just shook his head slowly back and forth.

Then I said something bold. I said it even before I thought it over. Had I thought it over I might not have said it. But it turned out it was good I made that request because it became a pivotal point in my life.

I said, "Show me my place in puppetta heaven... What I mean is – before you take me, before you take my life, show me."

Samael slid his right hand into the pocket of his trousers. He took out a little hour glass, somewhat smaller than the one I had seen in Papa's workshop. The top was almost empty. The grains were pouring down. Then he said:

"My time with you is up. I will return in two weeks and we will see what will be. When I leave you will forget about this incident completely."

I was back in my room. The time was 7:15. My heart was beating faster, but the bits of daylight scattered in the room brought happiness, joy to my heart.

11
Yossi's Pinhole Mirror

My Papa was more than just a woodworker. He had a special section in his workshop devoted to glass and mirrors. He loved to look at drawings of da Vinci's optics inventions. He told me he was trying to develop a mirror that would trap sunshine and let it out at night for light and warmth. But he was just at the very early stages of this. He knew it would take a long time – if ever – to see his dream come true.

But Yossi did invent a mirror that inverted the old Tuscan saying: "You can't have it both ways. A glass is either a mirror or clear."

He devised a little looking glass with pinholes. If you held it at arm's length it reflected your image; yet when held by your eye you saw through the pinholes. And more. The mirror was also a telescope through which you could see far away.

Yossi also told me, although he may have been joking, that on certain days you could also see things that never happened or even things that might. He said, "Some people call this the mirror of fiction."

When I asked him, "Is this really so?" he replied, "I'm not saying."

I could imagine he was acting like the angelic messenger who brought Geppetto the magic salve. More about this in a little while.

"Does this mean you can't say or you're not allowed to say?"

Yossi just nodded. Leaving me totally in the dark, in the mystery.

That pinhole mirror came in handy later when the local priest put Papa in a difficult situation.

12
First Meeting with Geppetto and—Nipocchio

A few days later, in town, not too far from the synagogue, I saw that puppetto with the adorable pointy nose whom I had bumped into the other day.

"Hello, didn't I see you the other day?"

He stopped, put his hands on his hips, and said in a surly tone:

"Actually, you didn't. Because if you'd seen me you wouldn't have crashed into me. But then I flew up to a branch and swung back down," here he stopped for a moment, "so how could you *not* see me?"

"That's why I knocked you down. Because I didn't see you. Had I seen you I wouldn't have knocked you down. And when you jumped down from the tree I did see you."

"All this is too much for my wooden head," the boy said.

"Mine too," I said. "But in any case, since this is the second time we've met, I think now it's time I asked you, What's your name?"

"Um...it's Nipocchio."

When he said that I noticed his long nose grew a bit longer.

"What a funny name you have," I said. "You must be joking. There's no such name."

"And what's your name?"

"Tinocchia."

"That's even funnier. And you know what? If there's no such name like mine, there surely is no such name like yours."

And he was right. Nipocchio didn't have such a wooden head after all. I shouldn't have made a negative comment about his name.

Just then an older man, short and thin, wearing rimless rectangular glasses and with a broad smile on this face came toward the puppetto. As he drew near I told Nipocchio, "I'm sorry I said your name was funny. And you're right. Mine is even funnier..." I waited for him to say something but he was silent. "Well, I have to go now. It was nice meeting you, Nipocchio."

The older man stopped. His eyes sharpened. He too stood with his hands on his hips. "Did you tell this young lady your name is Nipocchio?"

"Nipocchio is what she heard."

"Why did you tell her that, you rascal?"

"She crashed into me the other day with her little magic scooter table," the boy said, "and knocked me right up into a tree."

"What does that have to do with your name?" the man told Nipocchio angrily.

But to this the puppetto did not respond.

By now the man approached me. Then he turned to Nipocchio and said:

"Who is this girl?"

"Her name is Tinocchia, Papa... At least that's what she said."

"Hello," the older man said. He looked me over from head to toe. "Wait a minute. Tinocchia. I know you. You must be my friend Giuseppe's daughter."

"Yes, I'm Tinocchia."

Now the older man's face brightened.

"And I'm Geppetto. You probably don't know me but I remember when you were born. Your papa and I have known each other for years and we sometimes go shopping for wood and other supplies together."

"I know. I hear him mention your name."

Geppetto looked over his rimless glasses at the puppetto and then at me. "My rascal says that you bumped into him. Is that so? Did you crash into him?"

"I did. Quite by accident. He crossed the street without looking and I couldn't stop my little rolling table in time."

Now Geppetto turned to Nipocchio. "I still don't understand what got into that pine blockhead of yours to tell her your name is Nipocchio."

"I didn't say that at all. She misheard me. She's so excited meeting me again and apologizing for crashing into me the other day she probably misheard and switched some letters. I mean I didn't tell her my name is Abramo. People switch letters when they're excited. It's called a mental typo."

Nipocchio's nostrils flared and the tip of his nose got longer.

"What you've done, you naughty boy, is not nice at all. Is that the way you were upbrought?"

"See? See? You did it too." The puppetto jabbed his finger repeatedly at his father and began laughing. He clapped his hands in glee. "You did it. You just did it. Switching."

Geppetto gave a little snort.

"Now apologize to Tinocchia and tell her your real name. I am ashamed of you. Of your behavior. You should be proud of your name."

"Well, actually, I got so feduddled from the blow of her table I mixed up the pronunciation of my name."

At once the boy's pointy nose extended itself again.

The puppetto looked at me and then turned away shyly.

Geppetto nudged Nipocchio with his elbow and said:

"Go ahead, introduce yourself properly."

"My name is Pinocchio." And he gave a little mock bow.

Now his nose got shorter.

I regarded Geppetto. He was so lean a man he looked like he didn't eat. Short like most of the peasant men in the area, he had long brown hair touched with grey swept straight back. Yet his trimmed crisp mustache was white. He had a tiny stump of a snub nose, on which rested those rimless rectangular glasses that gave him a grandfatherly look. Geppetto was a bit gruff in a good-humored way, like an unplaned plank, occasionally mumbling about something that displeased him.

I felt bad for Pinocchio being criticized so often in front of me, so I said, "I'm sure Pinocchio meant no harm."

"Yes, I am a little mixed up since she ran into me," the puppetto said a bit sadly, and I felt even more sorry for him.

I think Geppetto was wise enough to gauge my feelings, for he said to me:

"Well, I hope you're right, Tinocchia. It was so nice to see you and please send your father my regards. I don't know if you know this, but your papa, Giuseppe, actually saw Pinocchio in my workshop before he was assembled. And seeing Pinocchio inspired your father to make a puppetta like you. Tell him he did a good job creating such a lovely and polite and considerate..."

By now Pinocchio stood behind his father and I saw him pursing his lips and making little faces and rocking his head like a cradle and sarcastically mouthing the words "polite" and "considerate," and then with wide open mouth miming "Blah, blah, blah..."

"...and well-bred puppetta like you."

Pinocchio was making me laugh and I tried hard to press my lips together. And, moreover, Geppetto's praise was a bit exaggerated, but I said, "Thank you for your kind words." Indeed, I had hardly said anything to mark me as well bred.

Pinocchio may have been a rascal but he was still charming, and his piquant, engaging face and perky nose added to his charm. Just looking at his face made me smile. And saying part of his name backwards and coming up with Nipocchio was quite adorable too.

Before he left, Geppetto turned to Pinocchio once more and warned him, "Remember, speak nicely to Tinocchia."

Pinocchio waited until Geppetto was out of hearing range. Then he said, rather proudly: "Do you know I'm the hero of a book?"

"Really?"

"Yes. Didn't you read that wonderful children's story about the rascally puppetto named Pinocchio?"

"No," I said. "I don't read children's books." *

-- --

*At this point in the manuscript another loose page was attached, with a different version of the last paragraph. The author's addition is on the next page. [Ed.]

[Here is our anonymous author's alternative reading:]

"Wait a minute," I said to Pinocchio, "if you're Pinocchio aren't you the hero of that wonderful book by Collodi, *The Adventures of Pinocchio*?"

"I am." And Pinocchio looked so proud as he answered.

"Doesn't it feel good to be famous?"

"The author could have done better. Too much preaching about going to school."

"Never mind that. What's important is at the end you become a real boy."

"But that's in fiction. The storybook world. You can't mix the two. I don't like make-believe. I like reality. What the author did for the character is between covers."

"Don't you want to be a real boy like you were in the book?"

"I'm considering it. My papa, Geppetto, has a way of doing it. I'll see. He says he'll do it for me if I'm real good...You know, since it's in the book's title, my name is always connected to adventures. I love them."

"Me too, but I haven't experienced any. Mostly I stay home."

"You can't have adventures at home. You have to go out."

"Wasn't bumping into you an adventure?" I asked him.

"No. That was an accident."

But soon I finally had an experience that was both an adventure and an accident.*

-- ---

*The author evidently did not resolve the little, almost insignificant, change in the dialogue about *Pinocchio*. Since he did not make a final decision, I am including both versions. Later in the mss we will again see mention of Tinocchia reading or not reading *Pinocchio*. Note too that the author has Tinocchia forget about the Samael adventure. [Ed.]

Curt Leviant

13
Beauty & Swan

One day, while Yossi went out of town for a few hours to do some shopping, I went down to the river.

I stood there looking around, all alone. The river was flowing gently; it had not rained in a while, the current was slow, not a boat in the water. What kind of adventure is this? I thought.

Suddenly, a swan I had not noticed before came out of the water. I looked at it and it regarded me. I had never before experienced a winged creature looking at me, staring at me at such great length. And then the swan waddled a couple of steps toward me. What a sharp contrast between its grace in the water and its awkward walk on shore.

Then, to my astonishment, it opened its beak and said: "Please wash my back."

Indeed there was a grayish stain on the swan's snow white feathers. Nevertheless, cautious, hesitant, yes, afraid, I refused.

Still, a talking bird was intriguing. Only in folktales had I met a talking animal.

For a moment the swan was silent. Perhaps I had imagined it talking.

But then the swan repeated its request. Again I said, No. I should have turned my back and gone back home. At this the swan changed its demeanor. Its voice became soft and ingratiating. The swan chanted a lovely melody rhythmically:

"Please wash my back and you will see, wash my back and you will see what I will give you, you will see my fine reward."

This chant, this melody, I could not resist. I thought of the fairy tales I had read. Maybe my washing the swan's back would break the spell it was under and, with my good deed, it would turn back into a human being, perhaps a prince. I dipped my hand into the water and began to wash the swan's back.

As soon as I touched the swan's feathers the swan turned – not into a prince, but into a beautiful girl, twenty or twenty-two.

My good deed worked. By doing the swan a favor I had released her from her enchantment.

But what I didn't realize until I looked down and saw my webbed feet was that I had become a swan.

"Why did you do this to me?" I croaked. But no words came out. "Is this my reward for a favor?"

But the young woman did not say a word. Perhaps she could not speak.

I waddled back from the river and up the street to the house where I lived. Seeing me, some little boys began teasing me. I think one of them may have been the puppetto Nipocchio or Pinocchio that I met the other day, but I wasn't sure for my eyesight was a bit compromised. Then I realized that by raising and lowering my big powerful wings once or twice the boys scattered in fear.

Oh, my, I thought. How am I going to try out for Queen Esther in the Purim-shpil if I'm a swan?

I waited by the door for Yossi to come back home. When he saw a swan waiting a few steps from the house he looked puzzled. He put down the two packets he was carrying and looked at me.

Again I tried to talk but I could not. Then I thought of humming, for I remembered learning that music was older than speech. So I began to hum a Purim melody we both knew. Of course, Papa Yossi recognized it.

Yossi opened the door, entered his workshop, and returned with a long thin stick. He whipped it in the air thee times and said:

"So someone's enchanted you, right?"

I was able to nod.

"And probably by the river. I still see the water droplets on you."

I nodded, a graceful, swanly nod.

"We're going to the river to meet your false double. It's probably a water imp."

With that long thin stick in hand, Papa walked briskly down to the river, and I followed at a slower pace.

The young woman stood there naked. I had never before seen anyone without clothes. She looked so pretty, tall, with a slim waist and long light brown hair. Yossi stood there as if paralyzed, looking, staring at her body. And I wondered if he would so be taken by her beauty he would forget about me. Maybe she would enchant him too to wash her back and turn him into a swan. Papa Yossi couldn't take his eyes off her. Even without moving I could see she was luring him. Then he shook his head, as if to drive alien thoughts away.

Papa had come to the river to save me – to somehow make her transform me to my original state – but meanwhile he was doing nothing. Just gazing at her.

The woman started slowly backing into the water; she began singing, no words, but she had a beautiful voice and the melody was enticing. I saw Yossi crossing the border of sand and going into the water. He dropped his long thin stick and began walking into the water, following the naked woman. I chanted the melody again but Yossi either didn't hear me or paid no attention. I went into the water and began gliding. I sailed between him and her. Gliding next to him I flapped my big wings, threatening him and, by so doing, I drove him back to the shore. Meanwhile, the woman, whom Yossi had called a water imp, was coming back. With my beak I picked up Yossi's stick and pushed it into his hand.

Again I began humming the Purim melody. I sang as loud as I could. He was hearing. He was listening. Now Yossi shook his head, two nervous tics. That seemed to break the spell.

"Come here," he commanded the young woman.

He swished the stick in the air. It sounded like a bolt of compressed wind.

She did not move.

"Step forward and wash this swan's back or I will beat the daylight out of you."

Still she did not budge.

Papa Yossi swung his stick in the air – now it made a sharp whooshing sound, like a wind warning before the lightning – and then struck the ground three times. Indeed, some sparks of daylight flew in the air.

Then Yossi addressed her, his voice as sharp as the wind we had just heard:

"Everyone has daylight in him to keep on living. Even you. We all have daylight and darklight. You, black arts, have more dark-light, but you still need daylight to live. If you don't wash her back right now" – now he pointed his stick at me – "I will beat the living daylight out of you."

And again he swung his stick like a whip at the ground. Now hundreds of sparks of daylight, tiny hard bits of diamonds, flew from the ground all about us, stinging slightly but with a pleasant, happy afterfeel.

Seeing this, the faux beauty quickly approached and began to wash my back. As soon as she touched my back our identities switched.

I became a puppetta again and the pretty girl a swan who rushed into the water and swam off gracefully.

"Have you learned your lesson, Tinocchia?"

"What lesson?"

"You broke the rule, Tinocchia. Don't you know you're not supposed to go out alone to the river?"

"But, Papa, this time you didn't remind me," I tried to excuse myself.

"And never, never do favors to talking animals,"

"But in storybooks they often do good things," I said.

"We don't live in a storybook world, darling Tinocchia."

I was so glad Yossi didn't reprimand me earlier, when I was a swan. To remain silent in a situation like that shows marvelous self-restraint. Another person would have scolded me right away.

"And I learned my lesson too," Yossi said a bit shamefacedly.

"What is that?"

"That girl was quite attractive. I was tempted to go after her and forget about you. But you acted very cleverly."

"What you did before, Papa, goes against all rules in folk-tales," I said, hurt. "You're supposed to rescue your beloved one and get even with the mean one."

"I told you we're not in a folktale," Yossi said, "but, as you can see, I did follow folktale protocol anyway."

For some moments we walked in silence, side by side. I wondered if anything of swan-ness had remained in me. Just then Yossi slowed down and walked behind me for a few steps.

"You know," he said, catching up to me, "maybe being a swan for a while wasn't so bad."

"What do you mean?"

Yossi smiled. "It did you some good."

"I can sing better now?" He knew I was joking.

"No. What's natural to the swan on water has helped."

"How?"

"Your walk. It's much more graceful. Like a swan floating."

Then I started jumping up and down and happily clapping my hands.

"What is it?" Papa asked.

"I'm so happy I'm not a swan. Can you imagine, I wouldn't have been able to try out for the part of Esther in the Purim-shpil."

I thought of sharing my adventure with Pinocchio, but I didn't know the way to his house, even though Papa could easily have told me where Geppetto lived.

14
That Man Returns

Just as he had surprised me the first time, he surprised me now.

"I'm back," said the man.

"Who are you?" I asked.

He just stared at me.

And then it all came back to me. And that fright, fear of him, returned.

Still, despite the tremors within me, I was able to say:

"I asked you to show me puppetta heaven, remember?"

Samael said, "I forget nothing."

"So what's your answer?"

I thought he would take out that little hour glass – but he did not.

"Stand next to me. No. Not there. No one is allowed to stand to my right. Stand to my left. Put your hand on my belt. In a moment we will ascend."

"Mr. Samael. Your scabbard is banging my hip. It's hurting me. Let me hold it."

I was sure he would refuse. If this were a storybook he would refuse. But as Samael himself said the first time we met this was not a storybook and he did not refuse. He unbuckled his scabbard and sword and gave it to me. I held the scabbard in my left hand. I thought it would be heavy and unwieldy but it was not heavy at all. I grasped his belt. No doubt the sword was just decoration for him. Samael did what he had to do by utterance and not by deed. I'm sure that is why he let me have his sword so readily.

I thought I would feel the ascent – but I felt nothing. That too surprised me. Puppetta heaven looked like a small town. As we stood on a quiet street. I took a few steps forward. I looked around. The place looked sterile. Little thatched roof houses, white and wooden, like in country paintings from fifty years ago. Not another living person in sight. Not a cat on the street. Nor bird in the sky. What proof did I have this was heaven?

"Where is everyone?"

"At work," Samael said.

I looked at him. I thought he was joking. But there was no smile – there never was – on the Dark Angel's face.

"Well, are you pleased?" he said.

"It looks all right. But if this is puppetta heaven, what's the difference?"

"There is no difference. The only difference is in heaven you know no one."

"And in puppetta hell?"

"There is no puppetta hell."

"Because we're made of wood?"

"No comment."

Perhaps Samael was showing me hell.

"Time to go," he said. "Now I'll take my scabbard and sword and we will go back to your house. This time, for the descent, I will wear it on my right side so it won't hurt you."

Again I spoke without rehearsing the thought first.

"No."

"What? What did you say?"

"I said, No."

A red blaze flashed in his eyes. The whites of eyes are sometimes bloodshot. But his were as red as fire. It was the only non-human aspect of his face.

"I trusted you with my sword. I showed you what I've showed no one before."

Yes, he was pleading. Samael was pleading with me. The sword was important for him.

"True. But this is not personal. It's not against you. I'll make a deal with you."

"People don't make deals with the Angel of Death."

"Aha! You said 'people.' Puppetti are not people. We're *like* people, but we're not people."

"So what do you want?"

"No more death."

He looked at me darkly. The severity of his straight glance was like a bore.

"Impossible. That is the way of the world. The earth cannot hold and feed so many people. Give me back my sword."

"No. I just want no more death."

"Death is part of nature. We're not in Messianic times."

"Perhaps we can start the process. I want to help it along."

"No. Give me my sword."

"Then give me a month's delay. In the Midrash Moses gets it.'

"You're not Moses."

"Fine, but then again how many—" I purposely did not say 'people,'— "talk to you directly like me. I bet I'm the first puppetta."

Samael turned his back to me. He seemed to be talking – but not in my direction.

Then I heard a voice that was not his.

"Tinocchia..."

Samael now faced me. But it was not he speaking. The words came in Hebrew.

"I understand what you are saying and what you want to do. But you cannot upset the way of the world. Samael does not work alone. He is under the divine command. Give Samael back his scabbard and sword, and he will accompany you back to your house."

I closed my eyes. I thought for a minute.

"He said creatures of woman born must die...I am not born of woman...Papa Yossi made me...I told him I am a puppetta and not of woman born. But Samael pays no attention to this and wants to extend his rule over me because he said that I live and speak.... So I ask you now, let us puppetti continue to live, since we are not of woman born. Then I will give him back his scabbard and his sword."

Samael had heard me. Now I waited.

I saw nothing. Not puppetta heaven, not earth. Just an endless blue sky.

And then I heard the cerulean blue words.

"I will take your reasoning under consideration and discuss it with my ministering angels. In the meantime, return his scabbard and sword. I will speak to you in forty days."

"Thank you. But I don't want to worry about this during that long period. Can you help me forget this scene? Like your Dark Angel made me forget our first encounter until he returned. As if it did not happen?"

"What did not happen?"

I couldn't answer that question.

Samael came toward me with his hands stretched out.

I gave him the scabbard and the sword. Now he donned them on his right side.

He took my hand and brought it to his belt.

I was back in my room. Just like last time it was still 7:15. My heart was beating faster, but the bits of daylight scattered in the room brought happiness, joy to my heart.

15
The Third Meeting in the Park

A day or so later, while walking in the town park, I saw a puppetto bent over a bench, rump up in the air, apparently looking for something. I wondered if it was Pinocchio.

So I stopped and asked him, "Did you lose something?"

He turned and straightened up. It was Pinocchio. My question seemed to surprise him, but he didn't reply. So intent on his search was he, he probably hadn't heard me. Maybe that's why he didn't even say Hello.

"Hi there, Pinocchio. Or do you prefer Nipocchio?"

He laughed and said, "Call me Pinocchio."

"I had an adventure the other day, but before I tell you all about it I have a question. Were you one of the boys teasing and throwing twigs at a lonely swan the other day?"

Pinocchio stepped back. "How do you know this?"

"That was me you were teasing."

"How? What?"

Then I told him the entire story.

He looked me up and down. "Wow! What an adventure. And you're all right?"

"As you can see. I'm fine."

And then his face fell. "I hope I didn't hurt you...I'm sorry."

"It's all right. You didn't hurt me. Now tell me what you're look-ing for."

"The gold tie clip my father gave me," he said. "I'll be heartbro-ken if I don't find it."

The puppetto looked so pathetic and lost.

"Not only that, but if he sees me without it I'm in big trouble. And I don't even know what kind of story to make up."

I looked at the puppetto. On this early spring day, a rather warm one, he was wearing a tie with his white shirt. But gone was the white cap.

Whereas the other day Pinocchio's voice was smooth and even, today it was nervous and edgy.

"Did you hear a little ping?" I asked. "Maybe that's where it dropped."

"No, I didn't hear a thing," the puppetto said.

"Let's do this systematically. We'll search in gradually increasing circles. I bet we find it."

"If you do I'll give you a reward."

"Not necessary. Let's begin." I made a mental circle and, slightly bent over, I began looking, eyes sharp, a mental image of a tie clip in my mind, hoping to mesh the mental image with the tie clip on the ground.

We looked for a while but could not find it.

"Wait! Are you sure it's on the ground? Maybe it slipped down between your shirt and your pants?"

"I didn't even think of that," Pinocchio said. At once he ran both hands down his shirt and to his belt.

"Got it!" he shouted. "You're right! Thank you. Thank you. You just saved me." And he showed me the tie clip with an oval loop in the back. It had been between the top of his pants just behind his belt buckle.

"You want to know how never to lose it again?"

"Sure."

"Next time you wear this golden tie clip take a safety pin and run it through the loop of the clip and attach it to your shirt. Nobody will see that safety pin and you'll never ever lose that precious clip again. Even if it slides off your shirt it will always stay on the safety pin."

"That's a great idea! Now you have to get a double reward."

"Not that I want one, but what do you have in mind?"

"I'm thinking about it," Pinocchio said.

I noticed the puppetto hadn't once addressed me by my name.

"Pinocchio, do you remember my name?"

He looked me straight in the eye. "Sure. It's that funny name that can't possibly exist, Intocchia."

Now I gazed at him. I didn't smile. Was he joking or had he really forgotten?

Then he broke into a broad smile. "Tinocchia."

I regarded Pinocchio's face and nodded slowly, my head assenting to my thoughts.

"You know, Pinocchio, you have a very mobile face. Did any one ever tell you you have an actor's face."

"Yes."

"Who?"

"You."

And Pinocchio, pleased with his repartee, broke into a hearty laugh.

He ran his fingers over his cheeks and chin as if he were looking into a mirror.

"Do I really have an actor's face?"

"Yes, like from the Commedia del Arte."

"In other words, a funny face."

"I mean it's a face that can make funny faces and make people laugh."

"Come on, don't talk in circles." He touched his nose. "It is a funny face."

"Fine. It's a funny face, but it's a fine face. Listen. Since you have an actor's face, I have an idea. Every year the Jewish community puts on a humorous show in the synagogue in honor of Purim, a tradition my Papa Yossi started years ago. Papa just recently announced in the synagogue that try outs would begin next week. Would you like to play a part in it? That is, would you like to try out? We need some lively young actors."

"What's Purim? I never even heard of it."

"A famous Jewish holiday in the Bible. Have you read the Bible?"

"Is it a children's book?"

"No."

"I only read children's books."

I noticed that little jibe at the snooty remark I had made last time we met that I don't read children's books.

"And one of the ways Jews celebrate Purim is by making a little comedy drama out of the story. In this play, which is called a Purim-shpil, the actors sort of chant rhymed lines. It's presented either in homes or in the synagogue. We put it on in the Siena synagogue."

"I know where that is. I pass it sometimes."

And then I told Pinocchio the entire story, which I had just finished re-reading, about the Persian King Ahasuerus, the evil Haman who wanted to kill all the Jews, and his evil wife, Zeresh, the good Mordecai who had once saved the king's life, and the beautiful Queen Esther, who finally revealed she was Jewish and pleaded for the lives of her people and helped save them.

"So would you like to try out?"

"But I'm not even Jewish, so how can I play a part?"

"You don't have to be Jewish. Non-Jews have also played in the Purim-shpil. And, besides, most of the characters in it, besides Esther and Mordecai are not Jewish... And every year there are lots of non-Jews in the audience...This year I'm going to try out for the part of Queen Esther. If I get it and you try out for Haman and get the part you can have dinner with me and the king."

Pinocchio drew back. "Wait a minute. I don't like that part. Who says I'm going to try out for that part? I'm not evil. I'm not bad."

"Don't you know the Commedia del Arte? The boy who plays the fool is not a fool himself. He has to be pretty clever to play well the role of the fool. Same with Haman. And with that role you get to be the center of attention, and you get lots of laughs. It's like the Commedia del Arte. Another wonderful thing about the Purim-shpil is that the actors can improvise. And so can you. You have a basic script but you don't always have to follow it or stick to the lines. That's one of the interesting and exciting things about a Purim-shpil. The improvisation. You make up your own rhymes."

"When is it?"

"It's at the end of March...The 25th. Are you interested? If yes, I can recommend you and you can try out. If the director likes you better than any other boy who tries out you can get the part."

"You mean someone else might be interested in my part too?"

I noted he was already calling it his part.

"Yes."

"Fine. Recommend me. Maybe it'll be an adventure for me."

"A safe one, don't worry. At least you won't be turned into a swan....And meanwhile, I'll give you the Book of Esther to read... You do read, don't you?"

Pinocchio stood straight and looked down the side of his long, pointy nose.

"What do you think? Of course, I know how to read. I go to school and read very well. But I don't understand a word of what I'm reading."

"See, you're funny already...Then you'll read the story and get to know it. And, like I said, the shpil is in rhymes, so you have to practice how to rhyme."

"I do that all the time," he said quickly. "Remember, when I lost my tie clip, you asked, Did you hear a ping? And I said, I didn't hear a thing...You see, I can do it. Now for your reward. You taught me about Purim, so now I'll teach you something."

"Before you start, Pinocchio, I have a question for you."

"Fine. What is it?"

"The other day, when you told me your name was Nipocchio, I noticed that your nose got a bit longer. Why?"

The puppetto blushed. He stretched out his two hands in front of his face, a gesture I would see him make often, and tried to push his nose back.

"You see, that fits right into the reward I promised you. What I was going to teach you. When I lie my nose gets longer."

"What do you mean, lie?" I asked.

Pinocchio blinked once, twice, three times. Then he said

slowly:

"Are you serious?"

"Yes," I said.

"You don't know what a lie is?"

"No. What is it?" I asked.

"You've got to be fooling me. You must," Pinocchio said. "Either that or you're pulling my foot." *

"I'm not," I said. "Why should I fool you? I don't know that word. What's a lie?"

"You really are a puppetta," Pinocchio said. "But now I'll teach you something about my specialty. You have to learn how to tell a lie. It's part of growing up."

"But what's a lie?"

"I can't believe this. This I cannot believe. You really don't know what a lie is?"

"No. If I did I wouldn't ask you. With the article 'a' in front of it it sounds like a noun. Is it a noun? Does it have anything to do with poetry?"

"Poetry?" Pinocchio was astonished. "What does poetry have to do with this?"

"Dante called poetry a beautiful lie, *una bella menzogna*, but I never really understood that remark."

"Who's Dante?"

"He's a cobbler who lives down the street."

Pinocchio just stared at me. He knew I was fooling. Or maybe he didn't.

"I'm just joking, Pinocchio. Dante is our great national poet. He lived and wrote in the thirteenth century."

"They knew how to write way back then?"

"Yes. Even thousands of years ago."

- -

*thus in the Italian: *piede* (foot) and not *gamba* (leg). [Ed.]

Pinocchio didn't know what to say to this; so he just mumbled, "Hmm."

"So now tell me. Is your word 'lie' a noun?"

"What's a noun?" Pinocchio asked.

Now came my opportunity and I felt so good.

"You really are a puppetto. I thought you go to school."

"I do."

"And they don't teach you about nouns?" I asked.

"No, in my school we learn useful things."

"Never mind. A noun is a thing, like wood, puppetto, nose, head, sky, water. Usually something you can see or hold. Do you understand?"

"I think so," Pinocchio said. "You say a lie is also a thing... but you can't see or hold a lie. It's not connected to your eyes or hands but to your mouth and ears."

"You see, I know the word 'lie' but it's not a thing, it's a verb. You don't know what a verb is either, right?"

"Right. I just go to a little country school outside of Siena. I don't go to a fancy school like you, Tinocchia."

"A verb usually describes an action, like to run, to play, to sleep, to lie down."

"Oh, I see," Pinocchio said. "Then my lie is not a verb. When you tell a lie it has nothing to do with lying down. You can actually lie standing up, like I do most of the time. You can even lie sitting down. Maybe next time I'll try lying lying down."

Now I was confused. I shook my head. "Lying lying down?"

"Look. It's easier to explain lying this way... For instance..."

And suddenly Pinocchio bent forward to my face, put his hands on my shoulders and kissed me with his tasteless wooden lips.

"...if I kiss you like this, and I ask you, Did I kiss you, you say...?"

"Yes."

"See? That's the truth."

"But what else is there?"

"Lies. Lying. My specialty. The thing that makes the world spin round. The thing that protects people from being blamed for what they really did." Pinocchio raised his right index finger. "Now pay close attention. Here's more of the reward I promised you. Now I kiss you again, like this, and I ask you, Did you like it, and you say...?"

"No!"

"You see, you learned already."

"What did I learn?"

"How to lie. Bravo. Your first lie. I kiss you, ask you if you liked it and you say, No, you didn't like it because you're shy, because you're a girl, because you don't want me to feel like a big shot, when you say No, see, that's a lie. Because the truth is, you *did* like it. Saying you didn't like it is a lie. Congratulations, your first lie."

"But it's not a lie. I didn't like it."

"Congratulations. Your second lie. Tinocchia, you're really getting the hang of it. You loved it when I kissed you."

"Now that's a lie."

Truth is, though I liked Pinocchio, I didn't like those thin wooden lips touching mine.

But that was too complicated for Pinocchio. For he frowned, put his finger to his cheek, and didn't say a word. He just kept staring at my lips.

After pondering for a while Pinocchio said, "You're getting to be an expert liar. Like me. But your nose doesn't seem to budge."

"But I'm not lying."

"Perfect. You're learning by the minute. Boy, am I a good teacher. Now you know what a lie is. Just remember. Don't forget. When you say something that's the opposite of what is so, or something that's just plain not so, that's a lie. Like when you asked me my name the other day and I said Nipocchio, when it's really Pinocchio. See, that's a lie, just like yours is a lie when you say you didn't like my kiss when you really did... Now if you come up with one more lie you'll get a reward."

"What kind of reward?"

"This."

And Pinocchio suddenly quickly kissed me again.

"Now that was good, wasn't it?"

I hesitated and said, "Yes," slowly – but I didn't know if I was lying or not.

Pinocchio made a face.

"Are you lying again?"

"You tell me," I said. "You said lying is your specialty."

"You know," Pinocchio said, "when I look into your eyes I get all confused. I forget what I'm thinking..."

"I thought you don't think."

"...and my mind turns grey and I forget what I was going to say."

As if to accent the point, Pinocchio stopped, and pressed his index finger to his cheek, by the side of his longish, pointy, impish nose.

"And, ah yes, I was also going to say I don't much like girls."

Soon as I heard that I thought: but me you're going to like, you pinewood rascal.

"Because?"

"Because...Because they can't do things that boys do, like kick the soccer ball...."

"...and lose golden tie clips which girls like me can find," I couldn't help adding. I waited a moment and then asked him, "When you said you don't like girls were you lying?"

Pinocchio stretched out on the floor. "Down," he said. "Yes."

The puppetto didn't realize it but he did give me a reward.

Now that I understood what the noun *lie* meant I was able to appreciate Dante's famous remark, "*La poesia e una bella menzogna*" – poetry is a beautiful lie.

Then I decided to give Pinocchio a reward.

I invited him to see a Punch and Judy show at the Commedia del Arte.

16
Tinocchia and Pinocchio at the Commedia del Arte

Just before the show began we looked up at a little box covered with wine-colored velvet curtains. Then the curtains parted and we saw Punch and Judy staring at us. The audience applauded and both puppetti bowed. Then Punch pulled something out of his pocket that looked like a playing card. He gazed at it, and Judy, curious, head atilt, eyes open very wide, as befits a puppetta playing to the audience, asked:

"What is that? It looks like some pictures are on it."

Punch replied: "They *are* pictures. This is a little machine that shows pictures."

"Is it a mirror?"

"A bit of. But it's different." Punch went into his pocket and took out a mirror and put it in front of Judy's face. "What do you see?"

"Me."

"When?"

"What does that mean? What do you mean, when?"

"I mean when do you see it?"

"Now. I see it now," Judy said hesitantly.

"Right," said Punch. "This little mirror is for now... But this little hard card is for later."

"What do you mean later?"

"Later means it shows you what's going to happen.... Like I'm looking now."

"Really? What's going to happen?"

"Look!" said Punch.

"Oh, my God!" Judy said and held her mouth in surprise until Punch bent forward, removed Judy's hand from her mouth, and kissed her lips.

"But I just saw that in that card," Judy said, pressing four fingers just below her lower lip. "That's why I held my mouth in surprise. That's what I just saw. How is that possible?"

"It's a special card. It's called instant pre-play. It tells you what is going to happen before it happens."

At once I thought of Papa Yossi's special mirror that he was trying to develop.

"Show me! Show me!" Judy cried out. "Show me what will happen next!"

Punch put the card behind his back.

"It costs a lot of money to use, and I'm running out of *lire*. So I can't look at the picture card any more to see what will happen next."

Punch turned the card around and looked at it.

"What are you doing now?"

"Looking."

"I thought you ran out of lire."

"But this part doesn't cost anything."

The audience laughed.

"So what do you see now?"

"I see what just happened."

"What?"

"This."

And Punch kissed Judy again.

The audience liked this and laughed again.

"Funny," Judy said.

"What's funny? Me or my card?"

"You," Judy said. "You have a funny nose."

Punch stared at her.

"My nose funny? I thought only Pinocchio's nose is funny."

Pinocchio elbowed my ribs, as if to say, Look! They're talking about me! See? I told you I'm famous!

Then the little wine-colored velvet curtains were drawn and the show was over.

The illusion of the puppet show was slowly vanishing, like the red glow of a sunset. It took a few moments, for it was hard to leave this make-believe world and return to reality.

17
After the Punch and Judy Show

I knew I was a puppetta but I didn't think about it. Which means that when I was outside with people I didn't consider myself different, and other people didn't consider me different. They didn't regard me as weird, invalid or freak. They didn't talk down to me or speak slowly as if I was deaf, stupid or a foreigner who didn't speak the local language. In other words, I was living as if I was in the real world, not in a folktale.

Because life in a folktale is – and here my favorite Dante line is useful again: "*una bella mezogna*" – a beautiful lie.

At the outdoor Commedia del Arte people didn't think it strange that Pinocchio and I were watching hand-held puppets. No one whispered, "What are puppetti doing at a puppet show?" No one exchanged glances as if to say, "They're enjoying their own kind." Even if they did they'd be dead wrong. What a comparison, real, life-size puppetti like us who could speak, think and write, actually high-class marionettes who were totally independent – and those painted-glove Punch and Judy Commedia del Arte puppets who were make-believe alive for less than an hour.

People thought of us as one of their own, even though we did not look like any of them. Neither did they question me as if I came from Africa or the Land of Ice. Questions I might have asked had I encountered someone like me, like, "Who made you? Where did you come from? Were you made this size or did you grow? How did you learn to speak? Do you go to school?" – they did not ask. Whether out of shyness or tact I do not know. That's why I think that people here assume that a puppetta is a natural phenomenon, nothing to arouse curiosity or prompt endless questions.

When I turned to look at Pinocchio for a moment, I saw an odd look on his face.

"You look so pensive, Pinocchio. How come?"

"If I knew what pensive meant I could answer. And if I were a liar I could bluff, but I stopped lying...most of the time."

"Pensive means thoughtful. What were you thinking about?"

Then Pinocchio said something that surprised me:

"About Punch and Judy up there...Even though Geppetto says we're marionettes we're not marionettes, for they're manipulated by people and strings and we're not. And we're not hand-held puppets either, like Punch and Judy. You and me, Tinocchia, we're unique. Nobody can tell us what to do. That's why I like the words, *puppetto* and *puppetta*."

"You read my mind, Pinocchio. That's exactly what I was just thinking."

But I must confess this, about me assuming I was like everyone else and everyone was like me. Once, suddenly, something happened to my ability to see and observe. Like a nearsighted person who puts on glasses for the first time.

Clarity came out of the clear blue sky when I noticed a young woman's beautiful bare arms. Soon as I saw those arms I thought I'd like to be like everyone else, and not have nicely made hinges for elbows.

But later I changed my mind.

18
The Purim-shpil Audition

I was so nervous going to the audition. I had prepared well by re-reading the Book of Esther. Of course I wanted to get the role of Esther – which girl wouldn't? – and Yossi too hoped I would get it. There was only one other part for a girl, that of the scheming Zeresh, Haman's nasty wife.

Unlike other years there weren't too many people here for the audition.

Another girl, rather pretty, not Jewish, read some of Esther's lines. She started fairly well but then stumbled a few times. It almost seemed as if deep down she rebelled against the Jewish Queen Esther's remarks and couldn't say them properly. Then the director, Salomone, who also played Ahasuerus, gave the script to me.

"Look it over, Tinocchia."

Just then I saw Pinocchio at the doorway. He could be shy and timid, I noticed, but now he sauntered in.

"Ah, another candidate," Salomone said. "You here to try out for a part?"

Pinocchio looked at me and smiled.

"Yes."

"Which part?"

"Esther."

Everyone laughed.

The tip of Pinocchio's nose glowed. I could see he was pleased.

"Well, since you're so funny, how about reading Haman's part?"

"Fine. I'm not here for money just for art," Pinocchio answered in sing-song.

Salamone answered, "Looks like we're in luck today."

"Just don't hang me at the end of the play."

Salomone chuckled; so did everyone else. I saw Pinocchio was staring at the pretty girl who had tried out for Esther's part.

"Well, well, well," Salamone said. "So you know the shpil is in rhyme and sung."

"Perfect for my forked tongue."

"And clever rhyming too."

"Even though I'm not a Jew."

Again laughter. I was so proud of Pinocchio.

"Anyone else here for Haman?" Salomone called out, then told Pinocchio, "Seems like you're the only candidate."

Then he turned to me. "Tinocchia," he said, "would you mind, if he – what's your name, by the way?"

"My name is –"

Was he going to say Nipocchio?

Pinocchio hesitated a moment, looked at me again and said: "Pinocchio."

" – would read a few lines first?"

"Not at all," I said. "It's quite all right."

Had anyone else come in I would have been upset at the director. Why should a newcomer who came in late for the audition be taken first? But since it was Pinocchio I didn't say a word. I was happy for him that he had made such a good impression.

Pinocchio approached and stood next to me.

Salomone gave him a script. "I see you're good at improvising, but I want you to read from the script too... By the way, do you have any acting experience?"

"Plenty," Pinocchio said at once. "In the Commedia del Arte. Can't you tell by my funny face?"

"You realize that if you get the role of Haman you play the part of an anti-Semite."

"No problem," Pinocchio said. "Some of my best friends are Persian anti-Semites," then looked at the script with a studious expression on his face.

"I'll let you study the lines for a few minutes," the director said. Now Salomone turned away and began speaking to some people who had come to try out for the Chorus.

"I love improvising," Pinocchio whispered to me.

I told him, "Salomone knows you can and liked you doing that. But first you have to master your lines. Actors are given words and they first have to say what they're given. All the more so puppettos. Just like in the Commedia del Arte roles you've played so often."

"I want to show I'm free," Pinocchio said. "I'm tired to being a puppetto."

"But in *Pinocchio* you say what Collodi tells you what to say."

"But I didn't like it. And today Collodi has no mastery over me."

I didn't answer. I nudged Pinocchio, telling him that the director was waiting.

"You have to show him you can take direction," I whispered.

And then Salomone told him:

"Once you have your lines memorized, Pinocchio, if you feel like improvising feel free to do so, but it has to be in character and in rhyme."

"Good. I'll go beyond plays, beyond puppetti, beyond books. And foo on everyone's nasty looks."

I didn't know what he meant by that. Sometimes Pinocchio's remarks were too complicated for my pine wood head. And, anyway, he had had his wooden head for a couple of years longer than me.

"All right, Pinocchio. No more chatter. Read."

He read well, with no funny or distracting antics. At once the director said, "You're an excellent Haman."

Pinocchio smiled. He smiled at me and then he smiled at the other girl.

"And now you, Tinocchia."

After a few lines the director said I was perfect for the part of Esther. This irritated the other girl, who obviously also wanted the starring role. She took, reluctantly and with grimaces, the role of Haman's wife, Zeresh.

This irritation was multiplied even more later.

19
After the Audition

I had gone to the audition alone. This was the first time in years Yossi hadn't come. I ran back from the Siena synagogue and told him that I had gotten the role of Esther.

"Today few people came to try out. I thought it would be crowded but it wasn't. And you know, the other girl who auditioned, she wanted Esther but she didn't read well, she isn't Jewish, she stumbled on words a few times, and got..."

"Hold it, Tinocchia. Wait a minute. Slow down. I can't grasp what you're saying..."

"It turns out she was upset she didn't get Esther but took the role of Zeresh, making many ugly grimaces."

Yossi nodded, as if he understood the entire matter. And then he told me:

"You know that the shpil's director, Salomone, is also playing the role of King Ahasuerus, right? That's been his role for years."

"I do know that, Papa, but here's something *you* don't know, and I'm sure you'll be surprised to hear who got the role of Haman. Guess who's going to be Haman in this year's Purim-shpil."

"I can't possibly guess. Who?"

"Geppetto's son, Pinocchio. He came, made everyone laugh by saying he wants to try out for Esther, and got the role of Haman."

"Perfectly fitting. I don't think a Jewish boy would have liked that role."

"And Pinocchio said he wanted to improvise, to show he's free, and not a puppetto who is told what to say, and the director agreed. But even before he read his lines he improvised a few lines in rhyme and made everyone laugh. He also said some of his best friends are Persian anti-Semites."

"Wonderful. It sounds like we're going to have a good Purim-shpil this year."

20
That Strange Feeling, Like Grasping Air

An indeterminate sensation, airy, like a tiny cloud within me, like a thought on the tip of one's tongue that has evaporated, a feeling like that plagued me, as if I was expecting an answer to a question I had once asked but had forgotten what it was, or as if I had to perform a certain task but for the life of me couldn't remember what I had to do – that was the sort of vague feeling that floated around in me. I could almost capture that thought, but like a fish in water it slipped away from me; that feeling was like a box laden with lead beyond my strength to lift, and I could not capture that elusive thought.

21
Zeresh and the White Dress

The time came to try on our costumes for the Purim-shpil.

All of us actors went down to the synagogue's storeroom where costumes from previous years were kept in wooden bins.

I picked out a white dress adorned with a little silver pin and draped it over myself.

I saw Zeresh making a face.

"You're too bony," she said. "It hangs on you. Let me try it on. Looks like it will fit me perfectly."

"But I saw it first."

"We have to do what's best for the play."

But I said, "I'm trying it on. What's best for Esther is best for the play."

And I tried on the dress and looked in the mirror. I liked the dress on me.

"Zeresh is right," Pinocchio piped in. "It is a bit too big for you."

"What do you know about dresses?"

I think Pinocchio said that because Zeresh was making eyes at him, and he, acting out his evil Haman role, dumb wooden pup-petto that he was, was falling for evil Zeresh's crafty wiles.

Meanwhile, I got out of the dress and was holding it.

"Let me have that," Zeresh said, snatching the dress. "After all, the queen is the queen, and the queen will look good in anything."

Zeresh tried it on. What was that evil woman doing with a white dress, looking like a ridiculous bride? I realized I was mixing the actress up with the character she was portraying, precisely what I told Pinocchio we would not do, when I suggested that he try out for the role of Haman. But I couldn't help it. She was acting like Zeresh.

And, yet, but, however, to my dismay, she fit into that white dress perfectly, and Pinocchio stood in a corner of the room with her, very likely telling her how good she looked.

Pinocchio was taking on the role of being Zeresh's loyal husband too seriously.

I didn't like that. That I didn't like. And I didn't like Zeresh stealing the dress away from me, nor her false, sly comment that Queen Esther will look good in anything.

While Zeresh was preening before the mirror – I could see she was admiring that silver pin on the dress – I went to Pinocchio, pulled him aside, and asked him why he was so cuddly with her.

"Because I'm getting into the mood of the role."

"But she's wicked. Even more than Haman."

"I know she's wicked and she's wicked Haman's wife. But don't forget I'm Haman."

Pinocchio tried to put a persuasive look on his face, and it almost worked, except for his eyes, which I saw right through, like a pinhole mirror.

I wanted to hold back the words, "How can I forget it?" but I could not. Sometimes we're split in two. The left side wants to be nice and forgiving, but the right is dying to get even. "Not a persuasive argument, Pinocchio. To get into the mood of your role, are you going to practice putting a rope around your neck too?"

To this he did not respond.

Later, on the night of the Purim-shpil, something strange occurred with Zeresh's dress. I know it's not nice to say this, but when I witnessed that surprising event it made me feel so good.

22
The Purim-shpil

I don't recall the entire Purim-shpil*, but I'm jotting down here what I remember, and I still have part of the script with my lines.

To begin, the director, Salomone, told the audience that a typical Purim-shpil is an imaginative take-off of the Purim story and not a word-for-word account. Hence, there is no such thing as a uniform Purim play. So then, although the basic story line is the same, the details and the dialogue change from year to year.

I should add that Papa Yossi was now in the shpil, taking the role of Mordecai. Salomone asked my father to step in because the young man who was supposed to be Mordecai had developed a sore throat and couldn't come.

Before the play began Yossi chatted with Pinocchio.

"So nice to have you in our shpil. I hear you're a terrific Haman."

Pinocchio did not answer. He just looked down and smiled shyly.

"You've come a long way, Pinocchio. I remember seeing you before your were born. When your limbs weren't attached yet. When you were in separate parts. You could have been stuffed into a big paper bag...."

"Not only one but two of those," Pinocchio sang out in the Purim-shpil mode, "the other, same size, for my nose."

Onstage, on the bimah of the synagogue, were all the players: King Ahasuerus, Mordecai, Esther, Zeresh and Haman. Since Queen Vashti disappears early on in the story the director decided

- -

*That Yiddish word, which means "play," must have been brought down to Siena from Jews who lived in Venice, which until a couple of hundred years ago had a Yiddish-speaking community. In fact, the very first printed Yiddish story book was published in Venice in the late 16th century. [Ed.]

to omit her from the play. In addition, there were a few people in the Chorus. Written in rhymed lines, the shpil was performed with a traditional melody that I hear within me when I write these lines, in an Italian sing-song very similar to the Commedia del Arte recitative, and similar to the exchange of verses sung on the street by the people during Carnivale.

Here now is the Purim-shpil we presented, with all the improvisations and asides.

Ahasuerus
    (aside)

I'm Ahasuerus, the mighty King,
(and Siena's shpil director,
editor and set erector).
When I speak – to attention spring!
Our Jewish Commedia del Arte,
a comic story, soon will start-e.
Here are all the Purim-shpiller
to play for you the great megilla,
so please sit still, and even stiller.

(Ahasuerus points to Mordecai and Esther)
    For our heroes a hearty cheer!

(He points to Haman and Zeresh)
    And for these villains a growling jeer!

(Haman and Zeresh retreat in fear and huddle in a corner of the stage)

Zeresh (steps forward)

I am Zeresh, Haman's wife.
Do I like stress, do I love strife!
But as for hate, it's Mordecai,
who with his clan is doomed to die.
Soon will come that destined day,

     Curt Leviant

(She turns to Mordecai)

So let all Persians shout: Hurray!

You'll see, when we claim victory,
you'll be swinging from a tree.

Mordecai

Ladies first, that's courtesy.
Try it, then report to me.

(Enter Haman)

Haman

All the world knows Haman's name.
The Book of Esther made my fame.
I am favored by the King,
for to his coffers gold I bring.
When Jews hear "Haman" they shout
  "boos".
What do you expect from no-good
  Jews?
No good will come from those
  He-buh-rews.
I just proposed; the King gave orders
to kill the Jews within our borders.
I'm not as bad as people say.
I'm quite okay; the Jews say nay.
My wife is worse. She's thinks she's
  Zeus,
that self-indulgent, silly goose.
It's Zeresh who should get the noose.

(Haman goes and hugs Zeresh. She slaps his face.)

(Haman whispers loudly, improvising)

I don't mean the words I say;
it's just the script I'm forced to play.

(I didn't like Pinocchio hugging her, but was glad that Zeresh slapped him, so I improvised:)

Esther
                    Follow script, stick to megilla,
                    you evil man, you mean gorilla.

Zeresh (to Haman, improvising)
                    You too are pine just like that strumpet,
                    whose wit and traits you like to trumpet.

(Well, that was news to me. That made me feel much better. How nice of Pinocchio to praise me to her. Unless Zeresh was lying.)

Ahasuerus (waves Zeresh aside)
                    You heard my name is Ahasuerus.
                    Pronounce it, please, as Ah-ha-swear-us.
                    I declare it all the time:
                    my name impossible to rhyme.

Chorus
                    One cannot rhyme a name so long,
                    Not in poem, shpil or song.

Zeresh (steps forward)
                    And don't forget my odd name too
                    the poets try but none can do.

     (she bows)

Chorus
                    Our loud and lengthy lusty hisses
                    to that evil brazen missus.

Haman
                    What a gorgeous name have I;
                    more elegant than Mordecai.
                    For my name too we have no rhyme,
                    a name so rare, a name sublime.

	Whenever I decide to choose, I'll rid my Persia of the Jews.
Chorus	Haman lets out hue and cry: to rhyme my name don't even try.
Mordecai	Why waste our precious Shushan time, with childish thoughts like, can we rhyme? Because of evil Haman's hate he decreed our people's fate. Since I refused to bow, he said, Soon all your kinsmen will be dead.
Ahasuerus	Look, here comes a delegation from the chosen Jewish nation.
Chorus (of Jews)	Oh great king, oh Ahasuerus, your evil Haman's out to snare us.
Chorus	Why claim we cannot rhyme his name? Those who do, they bask in fame.
Ahasuerus	An Italian proverb: rice is eaten in a crisis.
Mordecai	What link has that to the megilla, when we fear the Persian Titus?
Ahasuerus (shrugs)	It's just a catchy, rhyming filler. Injustice, yes, a moral stain. But a Purim-shpil must entertain.

(The King sees Esther entering)

Here comes my lovely lady royal,
my Queen, devoted, wise and loyal.
I love to have you, Esther, near.
What glad tidings bring you here?

Esther

No glad tidings, my dear sire,
but wail and woe, grief and ire.
My folk in danger, Ahasuerus!
The Jews, my kin, you'll have to spare us.

Chorus

One cannot rhyme his longish name,
no poet wild, no poet tame.

Zeresh (points to Esther, improvises)

Why'd they choose her for a queen?
A puppet skinny as a bean,
and made of hinges, paint and wood.
I should've been the queen, I should.

Esther (improvises)

But, Zeresh, you're not even Jewish.
You're mean, you're jealous, sly and
shrewish.
Your soul is made of wood, not love,
and Zeresh fits you like a glove!

(applause from the audience)

Ahasuerus (improvises)

Now, now, now, let's stick to script.
The Purim tale we must depict
in honest fashion, nice and strict.

Curt Leviant

Mordecai (to Ahasuerus)	Recall, I overheard a plot where plans were made to have you shot, but my good deed you soon forgot.
Ahasuerus	I'm so sorry, Mordecai! A foolishness that makes me sigh. Not giving thanks to my minister for saving me from men sinister. I for this lapse apologize. Here, try my signet ring for size. Although I'm called a demagogue I will build a synagogue In honor of my Mordecai, Who saved my life, who gave me *chai*.
Mordecai (inclines his head in gratitude)	Worse is Haman, Ahasuerus. With your kind help he will not scare us.
Chorus	The king's complaining all the time, His name is difficult to rhyme.
Ahasuerus	What's your wish, my chosen bride? To half my kingdom, long and wide.
Esther	To save my people, gracious King! That's the only prayer I bring.
Chorus (Jews)	Mighty ruler, Ahasuerus! Give us life! Free, declare us!
Ahasuerus	Who's the cause of this great sin? Point him out. I'll do him in.

Chorus (pointing to Haman and Zeresh, who point to each other)

Esther   Haman's plan to kill us Jews,
                                    that's his nasty, wicked ruse.

(Haman and Zeresh cringe, retreat. They do not huddle.)
                                    Haman, Haman is the killer,
                                    as we read in the megilla.

Haman   No, no, not me, it's all my wife,
                                    who has compassion like a knife.
                                    One thing, Jews, I must make clear,
                                    that your demise, that's her idea.

Zeresh (to Haman)   Then why'd you sign this damned decree?
                                    Hang him alone on this high tree.
                                    And while you're at it, Mordecai.
                                    It's time to bid him fond goodbye.

Ahasuerus   No, not in Shushan, this fine town.
                                    So Haman, Zeresh, fret and frown,
                                    your schemes they're now turned up
                                            side down.
                                    Evil Zeresh, cunning Haman,
                                    you wagon-draggin nasty drayman.

Chorus   Who says we can't rhyme Haman's
                                            name?
                                    Monarch does it all the same.

Ahasuerus   Prepare the rope, for two not one;
                                    the shpil is over, justice done.
                                    Hang them on the nearest tree.

Let Haman swing with missus Z.

Chorus
King even found a rhyme for her;
You did it, Ahasuerus, sir!

Zeresh (improvises)
You're a bunch of anti-goyim,
Jew-bilating on your Purim.
Anti-goyness is a crime
of which you're guilty all the time.
Don't like the way I'm being treated.
Once this so-called shpil's completed
I'll get even, count on me
and members of my family.
Revenge is in my DNA,
active always, night and day.
It's deep blood red in all my veins,
when it's sunny, when it rains.

(Chorus takes both Haman and Zeresh away to back of stage.)

Ahasuerus
With hopes that no one's been offended,
our comedy is now upended.
Finished now with our megilla,
we turn to drinking and *akhilla*,*
pasta, olives and tequila.
Yes, all agree that for the Jews
on Purim day it's fun and booze.

(Now everyone joins hands; Zeresh reluctantly)
We wish to every Jew and goy,
old and grown-up, girl and boy,
a happy Purim, full of joy.
Buon felice festivale,
gioiosa Carnevale!

- -

*Hebrew for "eating", and thus in the mss. [Ed.]

Just as the play ended and before our bows, I ran up to Pinocchio and said: "Why did you cuddle up to Zeresh, you dumb wooden puppetto? You see how she treated you, slapping your face."

"But that was part of the play."

"But you have to have enough sense to separate play acting from real life. I also noticed you made Haman less evil."

"I wanted to show how Haman was influenced by his evil wife. She should have been strung up in the megilla, not me."

"We can't rewrite history," I said.

"That's what storybooks do," Pinocchio replied.

After a moment's silence he smiled and said:

"You know, I wanted to add a rhyme about me swinging but I couldn't do it because it was too personal."

"Well," I said, "if you remember it I'd like to hear it."

"It ties in Haman hanging with when you crashed Table into me first time we met, but no one but you would have understood it."

Pinocchio took a deep breath, assumed an actorly stance, and continued:

> "It won't be long and you will see,
> I'll be swinging from a tree,
> just like when, instantly,
> Tinocchia crashed into me."

I laughed. "That's so clever, Pinocchio... You're a born Commedia del Arte star actor."

When we all bowed that rascal Pinocchio held Zeresh with one hand and mine with the other. I suppose he had to hold her hand for in the play Zeresh was his wife, but I can't forgive her for that anti-Semitic outburst, which she would very likely shrug off. But I noticed that Pinocchio, without looking at me, staring intently straight ahead, squeezed my hand quickly three times.

Now I felt better regarding Pinocchio and Zeresh.

During the applause Pinocchio turned to me and whispered, "Meet me by the water half past one. The weather's warm, we'll have some fun."

I squeezed his hand in assent three times.

But just before we left the synagogue an amazing thing happened.

As I was looking at her Zeresh's cheeks puffed; her face got heftier; her bosom expanded, her belly, waist and hips grew wider. In front of my eyes Zeresh was gradually getting fatter and fatter, blowing up like a balloon sucking in air. Then with a pop her dress exploded and, to my delighted laughter – I couldn't help it – hundreds of flakes of white cloth were raining, floating all over the synagogue. Something glinted in the air. That nice silver brooch flying.

As Zeresh slinked off, then ran in her beige slip, I looked for that silver pin on the floor but could not find it.

I should add that Zeresh's improvised remarks, calling us "anti-goyim" and promising to "get even" spoiled the festive Purim atmosphere for me. I didn't discuss this with Papa Yossi, for he would say that's her personality in the play. But deep within me I hoped these were just words and not a plan for nasty action.

23
Dogs & Chocolate

Pinocchio was late, so I strolled along the shoreline by myself. It was a warm, lovely sunny day. A big, furry white dog seemed to be snoozing on the sand. I had some chocolate in my pocket and, wanting to give it a treat, I put a couple of pieces on the ground before him.

But, to my surprise, instead of the big dog coming for it, from his white pelt a dozen or more tiny puppies the size of chicks emerged and at once rushed to the treat. They began to squabble among themselves, nipping and pushing and yipping in their thin voices, their in vain attempt at barking. They looked like ants swarming over and overwhelming their prey. And they moved so quickly and in so many different directions I couldn't even count them.

Despite their fighting they managed to devour all the chocolate. After the puppies had their feast they ran back into mama hound's pelt and vanished. Then the big dog approached me with a sad look in his eyes, as if to say: Is nothing left for me?

I bent down to placate the dog, whispered my regrets, and then turned and went on my way.

I hadn't gone ten feet when I heard a growling behind me. I turned quickly and saw the dog bounding behind me, apparently angry about the chocolate and seeking revenge. I pivoted and began running toward the water, and suddenly – there was Pinocchio.

"What's the matter?" he shouted. "Why're you running?"

"That dog is after me."

"Quick, let's go into the water. Dogs don't like water and he's too heavy to swim. I'll come with you."

We ran in and began swimming.

Pinocchio was right. The dog took two steps into the water, barked once, and ran away. We swam some more and then returned, dripping wet. I saw Pinocchio watching the birds.

"Look how they live by here in peace," he said. "The pigeons. The crows. The gulls. The tiny sandpipers with their quick tiny legs like racehorses. How they all stand side by side and one doesn't bother the other."

Pinocchio kept surprising me. I had never thought he could be so observant.

Now we looked for the dog that had been annoying us. He was nowhere around.

But as we walked home, slowly drying in the sun, there he was waiting for us. He approached slowly, not threatening at all, and from his pelt he took that silver brooch that had been on Zeresh's white dress before it exploded and rained bits of white cloth on the people in the synagogue. Evidently, that was why he was bounding after me in the first place.

Still, I wondered why the dog didn't give it to me earlier – unless he wasn't sure if I was the right person, but when he saw Pinocchio and me together, he realized that it was I who should get the brooch.

But how that big white furry dog got that silver pin (which I later returned to the synagogue storeroom) is still an absolute mystery.

24
Pinocchio Gives Tinocchia a Frog. 3 pebbles.
On Impulse, Tinocchia…

A couple of days later Pinocchio came to my house with a present. A frog.

I held it in my hand. It was a cute, placid little creature. I looked at it and, even though I thanked Pinocchio, I couldn't help saying, "What kind of crazy present is this?" I also couldn't help thinking of frogs as the second plague that overwhelmed the Egyptians in the Bible. One was fine, but not thousands.

Pinocchio shrugged, pressed his lips, and made a face I couldn't interpret.

"All right. If you think that's crazy, look at this."

From his pocket he took three small smooth pebbles, two white, one black, just a bit larger than lima beans.

"Here," he said. "These are for you. They're magic stones. If you rub them and make a wish whatever you wish will come true."

I had said something ungracious before so I refrained from any comment now. I just nodded my thanks and put the three stones in my pocket.

And then I added, "Listen, Pinocchio. I've been thinking about me and you being puppetti. So I want to, I have to ask you something. How do I know you're not my brother? My Papa Yossi may have made you too."

"No such thing. Where do you get that from? Geppetto made me. And then Collodi put me into his, my, book."

"What does that have to do with what I'm asking? You can't resist showing off about that book, can you?"

"Well, I just wanted to remind you there's two of me."

"One of you is quite enough. But let's go back to my original question. How do I know you're not my brother? Our fathers are friends. They've known each other for years. It's possible Yossi may have made you and given you to Geppetto."

Pinocchio put his hands on his hips in his typical braggadocio manner and said:

"Anyone who makes me doesn't give me away."

"Well, I still have to ask Yossi...It won't be good if you're my brother."

Then Pinocchio said something that surprised me.

"But doesn't the hero of the Song of Songs say to his beloved, 'My sister, my bride'?"

"How do you know that? Pinocchio, you sure surprise me. I studied the Song of Songs in the original with my Hebrew tutor. But you? How did you get to it? You actually read the Song of Songs?"

"How can I quote from it without reading it? Did you ever hear of an Italian translation of the Bible?"

The only response I had was a rhyme that came to me:

"Even though you're made of wood, to consort with you would not be good.... I'd have to look for another if you were, alas, my brother."

But the truth is, I didn't mean it.

And then that clever rascal, that Purim-shpil improviser, came up with:

"If I were a lass, how could I be your brother?"

And with that nice pun, Pinocchio, without saying another word, went to the door and was gone.

Then, to my great astonishment, soon as he shut the door the frog began to talk:

"I'm a lovely little frog, sitting here beneath a log. Green and clean, without a stain, I love sunshine, clouds and rain."

When I heard the rhyme, I thought at once that this frog might have been a good candidate for the Purim-shpil. What a surprise that would have been. But what role could it have played? Frogs don't appear until the Passover Seder.

From my readings in folktales, I knew that if you find or are

given a frog you're supposed to kiss it. But I hesitated, recalling what had happened to me with the swan. But then I reconsidered. If nothing happened to Pinocchio when he held it nothing will happen to me.

So I brought it outside, to the back garden, raised it up to my face, and kissed the top of the frog's head. When I put it down it hopped from one broad leaf to another, and then over a little puddle. Then it turned and, as its big, bulging, copper-colored eyes were slowly blinking, said to me:

"That was a very nice kiss. No human being has ever kissed me before."

I stared at the frog. "Well?"

"Well, what?"

"I'm waiting," I said.

"For what?"

I detected a bit of impatience in the frog's voice.

"For you to be transformed into a prince."

The frog gave out a little gargly, croaking laugh.

"Why are you laughing?"

"That happens only in children's books. The kiss that liberates the enchanted frog from its imprisonment. And who says, even if it would, could, happen, that I won't turn into a princess and make your eyes pop? It so happens I'm happy to be a frog. You think I'm part of a silly children's story? I was born a frog and a frog I shall remain, in thunder, lighting and in rain."

And with that it hopped away.

Later I told Pinocchio all about the frog, "Did you know you gave me a talking frog? And some of the time it talked in rhyme too."

"I could lie and say I knew that. That I purposely gave you a talking frog. But I'm not a liar. So I'll just say: What are you talking about? A talking frog? What kind of fairy tale world are you living in? A talking frog!"

I saw Pinocchio looking at my nose.

"Go ahead, dummy, measure it," I said.

"I think it's growing," Pinocchio said. He pulled out a tape measure from his pocket. "Still three and a half centimeters." He shook his head, grimaced. "Who ever heard of a talking frog?... In what language?"

"What's the difference what language? If it can't talk, what difference does it make what language it can't talk in?"

"Still..."

"In our language. In Italian."

"So what did he say?"

"You mean, what didn't he say?"

Pinocchio gave me a half smile. "Fine. What didn't he say in Italian?"

I came up with an absurd answer. "He said: 'Non posso parlare italiano'...I can't speak Italian."

I looked at the puppetto; he looked so cute standing there, confused, that I thought of kissing his cheek. "You remind me of that frog. Maybe if I kiss you, you'll turn back into a frog."

Pinocchio backed away from me. "Thanks, but like the frog, I'm happy as I am ... And, anyway, if you kiss me you may turn into me."

"No, thanks. As I said before, one Pinocchio in this world is quite enough."

"A talking frog," he muttered, looking up at the sky. "Absolutely absurd. What will she think of next?"

"So let me ask. How come a talking frog is absurd but not two* magic stones?"

"That's way beyond my wooden head," Pinocchio replied. "All I can say is in books magic stones have a long history."

I decided there was no sense arguing about these matters; so, without saying another word, I walked Pinocchio to the door. I

--- ---

*Note the discrepancy. At another point in the story, it is *three* magic stones. [Ed.]

Curt Leviant

thought he would say goodbye. Instead, he said: "You know, since I gave you the frog and the magic stones, I've been thinking about make-believe in the world of books."

Pinocchio stood with his hands on his hips, his usual pose when he felt proud and self-confident.

25
An Apology

I beg the indulgence of my readers (if there are any) regarding the brevity of this chapter. It is being written a second time, for the first version, a longer and more verbatim account, flew from my hand after I had written it outside one windy sunny morning, and the wind, being quicker than my wooden legs, made the pages take flight, and I could not retrieve them.

On those pages I related in detail the dream I had and the words I heard when God kept his promise to me and to answer, in forty days, my request, which I thought reasonable, and God seemed to agree, not to have puppetti subject to Samael's sword because they are not of woman born. He also agreed to my request that I should not have to remember this during that forty-day waiting period – for it would have been terrible to worry about this for almost six weeks – if I as a puppetta would live or would have to die.

But I do remember the opening lines of the blown away pages.

I woke that morning with that strange, vague, slippery feeing that I had dreamt but I didn't know what I had dreamt. That unsure, frustrating sensation lasted a while. Then, as though a script appeared before me, I saw the entire scene; rather I heard what the Angel of God was telling me.

In short, I heard from the angel that he was authorized to inform me that my plea for life was accepted on High and that my reasoning that puppetti are not of woman born is quite correct, and hence puppetti are not subject to the fate that is the lot of all humankind.

26
Pinocchio's Comments on Pinocchio to Tinocchia

"What do you mean?" I asked him.

"Well, regarding make-believe, I recently re-read my book," Pinocchio said.

"You wrote a book? I didn't know that. When?"

My enthusiasm, I admit, was a bit forced. I didn't think he could write a school composition, much less a book.

"When I say my book I mean the book about me. Collodi's book.... I still can't believe it's become so popular and famous. If you look at it closely you'd think it was written by the Italian Education Association. Every other page moralizes about the fix I got into by my skipping school. And Collodi even puts into my mouth pious words like: 'Ah me, if only I didn't listen to Lampwick I wouldn't be a jackass now.' I mean, isn't that boring? The same story again and again. How could the kids reading the book take this? But please don't get me wrong. Collodi is a marvelous writer. No doubt about it. And he deserves his world-wide fame. But he overdoes it. Am I glad I'm outside that make-believe book now and can take a more objective look at it."

"Do you skip school now, Pinocchio?"

"Me? Never."

I looked at his nose. It was quite the same.

"I learned my lesson from the book. You see, if you look at *Pinocchio* objectively, as only I can – I mean the book, not me – you'll have to agree it's not even that good."

"How can you say that? It's a classic, a world classic."

"I still don't see how it became a best-seller. Of course, I have no complaints. I became known, even better known than the book. But you have to admit it's boring and repetitive. In the book there are parts where Pinocchio forgets about his father for a long time. It's just not realistic. How can I ever forget Geppetto? And that baloney with the fairy, it just keeps on going on and on."

His remarks amazed me. I hadn't heard Pinocchio being so serious in a long while.

"Do you want to rewrite *Pinocchio*?"

"Not a bad idea. In fact, I was thinking of it. And you would be the hero."

"Me?"

"Yes."

"No!"

"Yes, you'd be the heroine."

"Would you give it the same title? *The Adventures of Pinocchio*?"

"No, I'd call the book, *Tinocchia, the Adventures of a Puppetta*."

"How about Jewish puppetta? There's lots of Jewish matter in it."

"Fine. A Jewish puppetta. *Tinocchia, the Adventures of a Jewish Puppetta*."

"But still, even so, even with such a nice title, how can my adventures, there are hardly any," I said, "compare to your many adventures? If anything is boring it's my life, not your adventures."

"Yes." Pinocchio said. "Ridiculous adventures. Go believe them. Becoming a donkey. Almost being fish fried. Saved by a dog. Only children and morons could fall for that. Me? A dancing donkey, tripping and becoming lame, and then I'm sold, thrown into the water to drown, and I turn magically back to a puppetto. And I hoodwink the poor guy by telling him the salt water did it."

"And the poor guy believed you."

"Yup. And my " – Pinocchio touched his nose – "didn't even grow. I told him that my good fairy sent a school of fish my way and they ate the donkey, tail and ears and all, until only I, the wooden puppetto was left... And Collodi, whom I never met in person, threw stardust into the eyes of kids and grownups alike and they believed everything."

"You don't much take stock in the magic of fairy tales, do you?"

"As you can see."

Pinocchio kept shaking his head in bemusement; he tilted it and pressed a finger to his cheek. He twisted his lips, a sour look on his mobile face.

"And then Collodi had a fish swallow me, shamelessly taking a page from the Book of Jonah."

"Of which you knew nothing about," I said, "until I told you about it."

Pinocchio didn't deny that. He just kept on talking.

"I don't know if history repeats itself, or stories repeat themselves, but I must tell you it just happened to me again. This time in real life. Not make-believe. Just the other day. Swallowed by a great fish."

Pinocchio looked at me, as if daring me to contradict him. I saw no movement of his nose.

"That's a fish story. A whale of a yarn."

"You don't believe it?"

Pinocchio held the tip of his nose with his index finger as if he was pressing it, pushing back against what his nature was doing.

"What are you, Jonah?" I teased him.

"That fish docks once a week in a lake outside of town and you can get a ride."

"On top or inside?" I asked.

"Inside."

"Nothing doing," I said.

"Don't worry. It's perfectly safe. Wood doesn't get digested."

Still his nose did not grow. Maybe he was telling the truth. Maybe he *was* swallowed by a great fish. Or maybe the mechanism in his nose had stopped working. Or maybe since this was one of his adventures in *Pinocchio,* he was just repeating it.

"I'm not joking. Next Tuesday. I'll show you the fish."

"I'll see it when I believe it," I said, then laughed. "I mean I'll believe it when I see it... Listen, since we're talking about adventures, your book, and the book you're going to write ... I might as well admit: I just finished reading *Pinocchio* for the first time..."

"Why'd you wait so long?" he asked, surprised.

"I don't read children's books. But for you I made an exception.* As I read it, I was astonished to see how gullible you were. How naive. You didn't realize when you met the paw-less cat again that it was she whose paw you bit off? And you went with them and followed their instructions and planted those precious four coins."

Pinocchio shook his head. He screwed his mouth into a disdainful grimace.

"So that's what you're reading, huh? Well, that's too bad. Books don't tell you the whole story. They just give the part that perks your interest, that satisfies the author's purpose. Like people, authors don't reveal all. They hold back too. It so happens, and it's not in the book, that I doubled back to the field and dug up the coins and took them back. So they didn't fool me after all. But for his book Collodi wanted it a different way, so that's what he wrote."

Pinocchio's nose began lengthening.

"And I suppose you presented those coins to Geppetto," I teased him.

"In a word – absolutely."

There it went, that nose of his, continuing its march forward. When would that growth stop?

"How about in a syllable?" I asked.

"In a syllable – yes!"

And Pinocchio's nose grew more and more.

I couldn't resist it. I tried to restrain myself but I could not.

"Pinocchio! Your nose is thrusting forward by leaps and bounds."

- -

*Again, a seeming discrepancy regarding Tinocchia reading or not reading *Pinocchio*. [Ed.]

"My nose is the outward symbol of knowledge. In a word, I knows it all."

I laughed. "You're a liar, Pinocchio, but you're delightful."

"So you see, I'm all nosing. The longer the nose, the greater the knowledge. With greater knowledge some people's brains get more wrinkled. With me, my nose gains weight."

"I think you've used up all your puns, Pinocchio."

"Maybe yes. Maybe not. Who knose*?" the rascal said, his index finger on the expected place.

Now Pinocchio smiled, delighted. He was so proud of himself, like a little boy. Even the tip of his nose, I won't say it glowed, but for a moment there was a beige, skin-colored life to it.

--- --- --- --- --- --- --- --- --- --- --- --- --- --- --- --- --- --- --- -

*An astute reader will recall that our author has already used this clever pun earlier in the mss. [Ed.]

27
Additions to the Purim-shpil

By writing down the Purim-shpil as I remember it, some more details have come back to me, One scene I recall is the dinner for King Ahasuerus and Haman. (I remember the lines, more or less, but only a couple of the rhymes.) At one point the King leaves the room and I'm left alone, reclining on a couch. Just then Haman approached and said in a low voice.

I don't remember if he said, "You're so cute, I want to see you alone," playing as if he were Haman trying to seduce the Queen, or if he said, "I want to see you after the show," playing as if he were Pinocchio.

And I answered softly, "Is this is a private remark or part of the shpil?"

But he replied ambiguously, with a couple of improvised rhymes: "Nothing is. We script according to what drives us, shy or bold, not according to what we're told. We try to best of our ability and think there's a difference between make-believe and reality."

Which words surprised me, for a) I didn't think Pinocchio could, or would, express such thoughts, and, b) I too had my views about make-believe and reality. I couldn't tell what Pinocchio's were. When he said, "We think there's a difference..." did he mean to conclude, "but there isn't any difference? Or did he want to say there *is* a difference."

"Anyway," I continued, "I'm not supposed to like you. You are Haman."

Now Pinocchio made his thoughts clearer.

"But you have to have enough sense to separate the me of me, the real me, from the character I'm playing. That's the difference between make-believe and reality."

I would hear similar views from him later.

Then Pinocchio and Haman seemed to change roles and

I heard, "I'm not really such a bad guy. I'm being pushed by my nasty wife, Zeresh, who frets and stews. Actually, some of my best friends are Jews."

I whispered to him: "I thought some of your best friends are Persian anti-Semites."

And then I said out loud, improvising, remembering what Papa Yossi had told me in the woods behind our house long ago:

"Haman, you were born on a bigotree and your wife on a harlotree."

At this the audience applauded.

I exchanged glances with Yossi, playing Mordecai. He was beaming.

Now Ahasuerus returned and found Haman kneeling on the floor bent over me.

"What? Will Haman now conquer my queen?" And the king gave a regal snort and said: "Off with him. Off with his head. Take this pagan, this believer in stone and wood, and hang him from the nearest idolatree."

"And what about his seductive wife, Zeresh, the one who prepared the gallows for Mordecai?" I said as Esther the Queen to the king.

At once Ahasuerus said: "She wanted to hang Mordecai. So we'll balance it out by hanging her. Let us send a servant to the woods and get Zeresh the tree she's fated for. For balance, let's find her the perfect symmetree."

A tree that Papa Yossi hadn't shown me in the woods in back of our house.

I should also include something that Zeresh said during the Purim-shpil, but I didn't want to spoil the good mood of the shpil by including it there. But at one point Zeresh added nasty words that were not in the play and were not even appropriate for improvising.

Zeresh shouted, "Death to all Jews and puppettos too. Puppettos are Jews and Jews are the Duke's puppettos."

And then Haman added, "But I'm also a puppetto."

To which Zeresh shouted, "That's why the king will hang you too."

That's about all I remember from the shpil. But I also remembered that on Tuesday next Pinocchio said the great fish would appear.

28
The Great Fish

Well, the following Tuesday I went with him and we waited at the edge of the water. We waited and waited. I looked at Pinocchio. He could see I was impatient.

"He'll be here," the puppetto said. "Maybe he's delayed. With the fantastic you have to have patience."

When the big fish showed up I couldn't believe it.

"Hi there," Pinocchio addressed him. "Want to give us a ride? I promised one to my friend, Tinocchia."

The fish blew some water from his spout and said, "No more rides inside me. I might digest you."

"But you didn't in *Pinocchio*," said Pinocchio.

"That was a book," said the fish. "And now we're not in a book."

"But wood isn't digested."

"Sorry. I'm not taking any chances. I don't want to be a fish filled with puppetti… But you can ride on my spout." And the fish blew another high spout. "It will be as if you're riding on a balloon. Except you'll be floating on water. Wanna try it?"

Pinocchio looked at me. "Well, what do you say?"

"No," I said. "I'm scared… But thank you, great fish." The fish looked at me, unblinking and sank down out of sight. By the movement in the water, I could tell that he had sailed away, leaving a long line of waves that folded into themselves.

*The great fish surfaced and said:

"I understand you'd like to have a ride."

Pinocchio turned to me and said:

"See? You didn't believe me. He'll open his mouth and we'll go in."

"Inside you?" I said to the fish. I was so afraid I was trembling. And I shook my head, indicating No no no.

"Do you think you can survive in me, like Jonah did," the great fish said, "and not be digested until there is nothing left of you but a savory sauce? No one can survive that. Miracles like that happen only in the Bible. Instead of being in me, you will sit or ride on my spout, comfortably, the best seat in the house."

And to show us what he meant the fish blew out and up a heavy stream of water, a sample of his spout. I liked the power and shape of this spout, but his fishy breath smelled like boiled carp.

Then I couldn't resist asking Pinocchio:

"How come a talking fish is okay, but when I told you about the talking frog you said that only happens in fairy tales?"

(I wasn't going to mention the magic pebbles because I hadn't tested them and don't know if I ever will.)

Pinocchio concentrated for a moment as if about to reply.

"You know, I don't have a good answer. If you had asked me this in my book, I'm sure Collodi would have put a clever answer in my mouth. But we're not in a children's book so I can't come up with a logical answer. But somehow with a fish's clever eyes and constant mouth movements it makes more sense for a fish to talk than a frog."

I was so impressed with Pinocchio's remarks both about his book and the way he answered my question regarding the talking frog that I did something unusual.

-- --

*This page is evidently an alternative draft of the previous scene where the fish says, "wood doesn't get digested." Moreover, here the author cites the Book of Jonah, which he doesn't in the other version. I can only surmise that he was still unsure which scene to use. [Ed.]

29
Tinocchia Kisses Pinocchio's Cheek

I bent forward. This time I didn't just think of it. I actually kissed Pinocchio's cheek.*

He put his hand there and pressed it as if to hold on to what he was feeling.

"Why that look on your face. Is something the matter?" I asked.

"No."

"Then why do you look so...so astonished?"

"Because no one has ever kissed me before."

"What? Not even Geppetto?"

"No. Sometimes he puts his arm around me and hugs me or pats my cheek."

"Did you like it?"

"Yes. I'm not like you and say No. I'm not a liar. Me, I tell the truth."

Pinocchio looked so pleased, so happy. I was curious about what was going through his mind.

"What do you feel?"

"As if I'm standing in front of an open fireplace but I have absolutely no fear that I'm going to be burned."

"Isn't that strange? You kissed me but you've never been kissed."

Pinocchio stood there with his hands on his hips, confident of the answer he was going to give.

"Do you remember, when I was teaching you about lying? As part of the lesson, I kissed you, but you weren't too eager to kiss me. At first you claimed you didn't even like it.... Although when I kissed

--- --- --

* The author evidently forgot that in an earlier chapter Tinocchia has already kissed Pinocchio. [Ed.]

you the second time and asked you if you liked it, you sort of said, Yes, although you very cleverly said you didn't know if you were lying or not."

"Yes. That was something new and strange... You know what, Nipocchio?"

"You said Nipocchio?"

"Did I?"

"Yes, you did."

"I did it purposely," I said with a flirtatious tone. "Quite purposely... Yes, let's try it again. Maybe I'll like it this time."

Pinocchio put his arms around my back and drew me close. I closed my eyes, just like the heroines in the books I had read. I could smell the nicely polished pine wood of his face. He kissed me again.

He was silent for a moment, as if waiting for me to speak. I guess he wanted a reaction from me.

"Well," the puppetto said finally. "Did you like it?"

"Yes," I said.

"You're not lying?"

"No."

"See!"

But the truth is I didn't like it that much. I was sort of fibbing. I liked Pinocchio. I enjoyed his affection. But his lips on mine? Maybe I would have to practice more. But I had to become Pinocchio for a moment and lie so as not to hurt his feelings.

It was then that I realized that truth and lies were not strictly opposite like black and white. There were lots of shadings between the two poles. And I also realized that lies could sometimes be used to make someone feel good.

But yet it was because of his constant lying that I didn't believe Pinocchio when he gave me his magic pebbles. I was sure it was another one of his bluffs.

Let me explain:

I was alone in the house, making order in the kitchen. In the back of the dish cabinet I re-discovered a little glass jar with the three smooth oval stones, two white and one black, that the pup-petto had given me. He said if I held all three stones in my hand they would take me anywhere.

And his nose did not get any longer when he said this.

Well, when I was alone I did this and nothing happened.

So when I saw him next time I said:

"You told me those stones you gave me are magical, but they are not. I held them in my hand and nothing happened."

"Which hand did you hold them in?" Pinocchio asked.

"In my left."

"No wonder. It should've been your right."

"You didn't tell me," I said.

"You didn't ask. People usually hold things in their right hand."

"I need my right hand," I said, "to open doors, to write, to do things."

"Next time, keep them in your right hand. They'll work. Guar-anteed."

Well, that rascal was constantly surprising me.

30
Looking at Clouds and Flying Up

When the clouds in the sky enchanted me in various shades of blue and grey, I would stop what I was doing and look at that wide expanse above. I liked the way the clouds floated lazily, thin and thick, and slowly changed their shape. At times I saw elongated dogs or dragons with tails dark grey and green and white, or just plain puffy clouds set against a blue sky that made me feel so good. Then even the tops of black clouds were edged with pink. Once I saw a cloud shaped like a long goose feather; another time like a long thin transparent wispy fish. The magic was especially impressive as the day faded, when parts of the blue sky were tinged with green and stripes of orange, red and pink appeared between the clouds.

One day I was looking up at a lone huge puffy white cloud and, it seemed to me I saw the first letter of my name among the spaces appearing in the formerly solid cloud. And then I wondered why I, if flying in a balloon, couldn't grasp a cloud and continue my journey that way.

In my pocket I had the three smooth pebbles, two white, one black, Pinocchio had given me that he claimed were magic stones. Even though I didn't believe him, I held the stones in my right hand, rubbed them, and imagining myself in the cloud, said aloud anyway:

"I wish I could ride in a cloud for a few minutes and see what the cloud sees."

I don't know if I heard the words, "All right", or if I just imagined them, but at once I felt myself being sucked up by a wind. Then, as if in a waking dream, I was holding on to two ropes of a swing and sitting on a little wooden board. I noticed a little extra piece of rope no longer than Pinocchio's nose dangling on a thread. I pulled at it so the ropes would look balanced on both sides, and I put that tiny bit of rope in my skirt pocket.

As I swung back and forth, I looked down at Tuscany and

saw the hills and valleys and the green countryside with patches of forests and the river and the plots of land where the farmers grew their wheat and vegetables, even the red brick of Siena and the great square and the spires of churches. As I floated in the cloud I imagined myself painting this scene. What a beautiful work of art that would have been.

While I was up in the clouds, feeling as if I was in a waking dream, or perchance asleep, a question came to me. One I had always pondered: at what point do we fall asleep? Exactly where is the border, that thin fine line, between waking and sleep? Will I ever be able to experience that moment and say to myself, yes, here, at this point, I am sleeping?

Then I put my hand into the other pocket of my skirt and realized that I had taken Yossi's little pinhole mirror. I looked through it and saw our house, the garden in back, and the woods behind it. And then I saw something I liked and something I didn't like. Papa Yossi had hinted that with this magic mirror we could also sometimes see events before they happened. But he didn't say it pictured events that had taken place. Now I suddenly saw myself as Esther in the Purim-shpil. And then the picture changed and I saw Pinocchio cuddling up to Zeresh.

That annoyed me. I was upset. On the other hand, why should I be angry with someone for a past deed, just because of a little mirror? Maybe my jealousy *made* me see this little picture, as if from a telescope.

But then something else distracted me. I suddenly heard a man's voice clearly speaking to me. This surprised me for up here in the clouds who could possibly be talking to me?

He said: "Can you hear me?"

"I hear you but I can't see you."

"There's no need to see me. Just listen. You have been chosen to get three wishes."

"This sounds like something out of a fairy tale."

But to this remark the voice did not respond.

Then I asked, "Why did you choose me?"

"You're asking too many questions."

"Some time ago, when I spoke to Samael, he answered my questions."

"Ah! First of all I'm not Samael. Samael is different. Him you get to see only once. But you seem to have survived that meeting. But types like me you can see often without any problems. Just don't ask so many questions."

I wanted to tell him I was brought up to ask questions but I kept silent.

"I don't do the choosing," he finally said.

Was this connected to something I had done? Like helping a girl with her homework in my class? Or carrying a heavy bundle the other day for an old lady? Or was this a mistake?

"Well, I'm waiting," the man said. "You're not going to be up here much longer. Tell your three wishes."

I had to think quickly.

"Wish number one, a good life for Yossi."

"Done."

"Wish number two, a good life for Geppetto and Pinocchio."

"Done."

Now I hesitated for a moment.

"And your third wish."

"My third wish – "I began hesitantly, knowing that my third wish is going to be highly unusual.

"Wait a minute!" The man interrupted me. "You're actually – "

"You already know my third wish without even me saying it?"

"I know everything."

"My third wish is for three more wishes..." I said in a rush of words.

"Nothing doing. This goes against the tradition of every folktale."

But I paid no attention to him; I just muttered, "I'm not bound to the folktale world. You gave me three wishes. Where is it written that my third wish can't be for three more wishes?

"It's never been done before."

"It's not my fault that characters in folktales don't have imagination...So that's my third wish. But I'm going to hold those extra wishes in abeyance."

"What does that mean?"

"Look it up." So he really *doesn't* know everything, I thought.

"But you're going to have to take your extra wishes right now."

"No. But I'll tell you what. I'll compromise with you... I'll do two of them right now. My first wish is that the Jews in our community and in the rest of the world continue to live in peace. And the second is that my memoir, this book, gets published and becomes as well-known as *Pinocchio*."

I noticed, and it didn't please me, that whereas he said, "Done" for the first two wishes, now for my extra ones he did not say "Done".

About this I didn't ask him. I sensed that I had pushed him enough.

"And the third wish?"

"I told you. Some other time."

But then the time span of my up-in-the-clouds flight must have ended, for I heard the reverse insuck of wind and I had to let go of the ropes I was holding, and with a rush of noise and closed eyes I floated down quickly back to earth.

I couldn't wait to tell Yossi and Pinocchio what happened to me, but I knew they wouldn't believe me. Then I remembered I had a piece of the sky rope in my pocket; I would show that as proof of my adventure.

Even with that Pinocchio would think I was lying.

Thinking about this I pictured the puppetto and his wondrous nose.

And, with a surge of joy that made my eyes open wide, I remembered that I still had one wish left. Could I extend those wishes indefinitely?

31
Tinocchia Analyzing Growth of Pinocchio's Nose.

There are a couple of ways of analyzing how Pinocchio's nose grew.

Was it just extra wood added to the tip? If so, then the area of elongation would be seen. There would be a tiny mark in the wood, in the spot from which the new growth would – a nice, accidental, pun – start. Or did the growth come about in a different way? It involved the whole nose, from beginning to end, and each pine cell played its part in the expansion process – like a child's hand growing.

Or am I going about it the wrong way? After all, Pinocchio's nose getting longer when he lied is something fictive, magical, beyond the real. Still, his pinewood nose growing came about as naturally as God's two-word Hebrew command at Creation, "*Yehee" or,* – "Let there be light." Go analyze *that* from a realistic point of view.

Pinocchio's nose growing reminded me that Papa Yossi once told me:

"Reading Italian and English from left to right and Hebrew from right to left when one is young helps your brain develop and grow."

And that made me wonder what brain power, if any, was involved with Pinocchio's nose. What a stroke of genius of Collodi to have Pinocchio's nose grow when he lied. And even when Pinocchio left the make-believe world of books in *Pinocchio* and became a puppetto in the real world he kept that attribute. Pinocchio probably didn't like that, but there was nothing he could do about it. He made the best of it and, on occasion, even bragged about this unique quality.

And there was another thing he bragged about: believe it or not, grammar and language.

32
Pinocchio's Grammar Lesson

Pinocchio said to me, "If you are a marionette, I am a marion. If you are—and indeed you are—a cocquette, then I am a cocq. If I am a puppetto, you are a puppetta."

"Even according to the rules of Hebrew grammar," I said. "You see, also in Hebrew, when you add *ah* to a masculine noun it makes it feminine."

"That language is totally foreign to me. I only know Latin and Greek. And grammar. And maybe another language or two."

I didn't even have to look. I knew what was happening above his lips, below is eyes.

"And anyway, Pinocchio, how come you suddenly know so much about grammar? You didn't even know what a noun was. Or a verb."

"One. I'm a good guesser. Two. I know Azerjibanian. Which you don't know."

"You don't even know how to pronounced it. You mean Azerbijanian."

"That's what I meant. And you didn't know that I know it. Azerbijanian is like Albanian but longer. Azerbijanian is easy. Perfect for an amateur grammarian like me. It's the only language I know without nouns or verbs. It has a very limited vocabulary. In fact, most of the words in Azerbijanian are Yes, No, Up, Down, Right, Wrong, Windowshade, Me, You, and And."

"Where is Azerbijan?"

"I don't know....It may not even exist anymore. How can a country exist on ten words?"

"You said that language doesn't have nouns. 'Windowshade' is a noun."

"There are exceptions in every language. Grammar is based on exceptions."

"And how come they have such a useless word like window-shade as their only noun? Not even bread?"

Pinocchio gave me such a pitying look, as if I were some kind of dullard.

"When you undress at night and there's a window in your room, what would you rather have, a windowshade or bread?"

"I see your point."

I knew Pinocchio was spoofing, bluffing, but still I kept encouraging him, seeing how far he would take his exaggerations.

"Can you speak Azerbijanian?"

"No one can. It's a written language."

"So then how do they communicate?"

"By writing and lots of nodding. Endless nodding. That's why so many Azerbijanians suffer from stiff necks. In a language with limited vocabulary, word order is crucial. Me You Down has a different meaning than Down Me You."

I kept on teasing him but he didn't realize it. He was off in a world of his own.

"So what do those phrases mean?"

"I don't know. I told you I don't speak Azerbijanian."

"You mentioned grammar. So I assume this language has lots of grammar."

"Lots."

"Give me an example."

"All right. For instance, the word 'and' can be singular, plural, somewhere in between, and even zero. It's one of the mysteries of Azerbijanian grammar, which I told you is one of my specialties."

"And what's the other?"

Clever Pinocchio brought his index finger to his pointy nose, which during this conversation kept getting longer and longer. I suppose he wanted to indicate that his nose is his other specialty.

"Pinocchio, does your nose get any longer than this?"

"Sometimes. In fact, my nose used to be so long two boys could hold on to it and swing from it as if on parallel bars."

"Really?"

"Word of honor."

At once the proboscis extended itself; now three little liars could easily swing from it.

"Pinocchio, you have such a great imagination. You should be a writer. You could write a book."

"I did. It's called *Pinocchio*."

"Are you working on anything else? Another book?"

"Yes."

"What?"

"This one."

33
Stealing One's Heart

Suddenly, Pinocchio said, "I want to steal your heart."

I brought my hands to the golden heart hanging from my necklace. It wasn't really gold, just tinsel. But it looked like gold. Why did Pinocchio say that? Did he want to take it? I didn't understand what that expression really meant until much later, when I repeated what he said and commented:

"Like the fox and the cat who wanted to steal your five gold coins?"

"How do you know about that?"

"Oh, I heard," I said vaguely. I didn't want to admit I had read all about this in the *Adventures of Pinocchio* after telling him I don't read children's books.*

"No." Pinocchio smiled. "No, not like those two nasty creatures... Why do you ask?"

"I'll tell you straight out," I said, rather severely. "Isn't lying enough of a fault? You want to add stealing to your list of misdeeds?"

"You silly puppetta," Pinocchio chided me. "Sometimes I think you have even more of a wooden blockhead than me. Stealing one's heart is just an expression. It means..." and Pinocchio placed his right hand on his heart and removed it slowly in a broad arc in quite a grandiloquent, ballet-like gesture. No words were necessary. I understood every word he didn't say.

- -

*Here we have another instance where our anonymous author did not decide on two contradictory statements: whether Tinocchia read or did not read *The Adventures of Pinocchio*. Moreover, the number of planted coins mentioned in Chapter 19 is four. [Ed.]

34

Each Time Pinocchio Lies, Tinocchia's Nose Gets Longer, Says Pinocchio

"Do you like me?" Pinocchio asked.

"Well, sort of," I said hesitantly.

I looked at his face. Something strange was happening.

"Why is your nose longer, Pinocchio?"

"Is it?"

"Yes. It is."

He touched his nose.

"Terrific," Pinocchio said, "You're getting the knack of lying. Each time you lie my nose gets longer."

He looked at me; rather, stared at my nose. "If you'd've said Yes and told the truth, my nose would stay where it was."

I touched my nose. "Maybe some sort of magical switch is taking place. Now, every time you lie, *my* nose gets longer."

35
Pinocchio's Gift of an Eagle Feather to Tinocchia

The next time Pinocchio came over he said:

"Okay, Tinocchia, since you shared with me the magic mirror, even though I couldn't see myself in it, today I am going to give you something..."

And he began to tell me how he was in a forest once and met up with four creatures who were standing around a dead donkey, a lion, an ant, a dog and an eagle.

"Are you sure," I asked him, "you're not telling me a story from some book of folktales?"

"Not at all. This really happened. They saw me standing there watching them and looking at the dead donkey, so they asked me to divide the donkey for them. I looked at the dead animal and made my decision.

"I gave the head to the ant, the hooves to the dog, the entrails to the eagle, who could take it up to the highest tree and feast on it, and the rest to the biggest animal with the biggest appetite, the lion. They all seemed to be satisfied with the way I divided the dead donkey because for a moment they stopped eating and huddled together as if conversing. Then the eagle approached me, plucked a feather from its body with its beak, and said, 'We have decided to reward you for your wisdom. Here, take this feather. Whenever you want you can hold this feather and make a wish on it and it will turn you into the most powerful eagle that can fly anywhere.' And now I am giving this feather to you, Tinocchia."

Since Pinocchio's three magic pebbles did work, when I wished to be up in the clouds, I didn't doubt him this time, but I really didn't want to be transported anywhere now. However, I took the feather anyway. I should add that Pinocchio told the story beautifully, as if he had composed it himself. But I'm sure he didn't. Perhaps something from Collodi had rubbed off on him. Or some folktale he had heard or read somewhere.

When I returned home, I casually flipped that so-called magical eagle feather into a corner of the little riding box atop of Table.

What we experienced next was neither a folktale nor magical, for that morning there was a big white envelope in our mailbox.

The big black cross on the left top puzzled us and made us nervous.

"Who from the church would be writing to us?" Yossi wondered. "And why?" Now there was a quaver in his voice. "I don't like the looks of this envelope."

36
Before the Signs Debate. Summoned By Priest

"Come here, Tinocchia," Papa Yossi called. There was a tremor in his voice I had not heard before. As if his voice had become a vibrating string. "Look at this. It's a letter from Antonio, the head priest of the Siena church."

It has come to our attention that you presented a play recently in the synagogue that maligned Christianity. We are not pleased that the Jewish community presented such an anti-Christian spectacle. In view of this, you are summoned to the church to discuss this matter of utmost importance with me.

Father Antonio

"What nonsense!" Papa shouted. "Anti-Christian! What a boor!" He crumpled the note and threw it at the wall. "He's too ignorant to realize that the megilla was written centuries before Christianity was born... Who do you think could have brought our Purim-shpil to the priest's attention?"

Now Yossi paced in the room. He didn't shout but he spoke loud enough. "The non-Jews who attended were ones who have come before in previous years and they understand the story. They laugh and the enjoy the play. Who could have done this?"

"I can't imagine who," I said almost automatically, but then someone did come to mind.

"Do you think it could have been...?" Papa said slowly. "No, I can't imagine that he... I don't even want to say..."

"No, Papa Yossi. Don't even think of it. He's naughty but not mean. He'd never do something like that, even though he played Haman."

"Then who could it be?" Papa asked. "Someone obviously told the priest about our shpil."

Then I said it aloud. "Now that I think of it. It fits her. It fits her role. The other non-Jew in the Purim-shpil. Zeresh. It has to be her. Remember, she even improvised some remarks that fit her role."

"Yes, I remember that, but I passed it off as role playing."

"I knew you would say that, Papa, but those were strong words. She said she'd get even. And nasty words like, death to Jews and puppets too... It's Zeresh. Who else could it be?"

Yossi nodded slowly. "Perhaps you're right."

"It is her. Why did she even bother to take a role in the first place? Unless she did it purposely in order to tattle."

Yossi put his hands on my shoulders.

"Tinocchia, even if you're right, we can't jump to conclusions. We have no proof. It could have been someone from the audience."

"But you know, Papa, it doesn't make much difference now. What are you going to do about the priest's note?"

Yossi picked up the letter, straightened it, and looked at it again.

"I have no choice. I'll go talk to him. If I ignore his note it's almost as if I agree with him and have something to hide."

"Papa, do you think we should consult Rabbino dei Rossi?"

"Absolutely not. I won't even tell him. As far as I'm concerned this is a minor matter. Let's save rabbinic intervention and influence for something more serious."

Soon as he said this, I remembered that Giorgio, the Mayor of Siena, was Papa's friend. Since Yossi didn't want a religious leader to intervene, perhaps he would ask the mayor. But I decided to keep still. If Papa didn't mention it I wouldn't either. But I did say:

"You know, maybe Zeresh wants revenge."

"For what?"

"For the insults I improvised against her. On the other hand," the thought came to me, "she knew the role she was going to play. Maybe she's mad because she didn't get the part of Esther."

"Tinocchia, it's hard to examine the heart of another. There are always surprises... But let's first go to the priest and see how my talk with him goes."

"Can I come with you?"

"Of course."

The priest opened the door. This was the first time I'd ever seen him. Antonio was robust, on the short side, with an oblong face and thin bluish lips that didn't make him look very friendly. But he surprised us by receiving us cordially. He even was the first to extend his hand in welcome. At once Papa Yossi told him, "Sir, I received your letter and I'm glad to have the opportunity to speak with you. But I want you to know that your assumption is totally mistaken. You were not in the synagogue, you did not hear the play, which quite a number of your fellow Christians come to every year and enjoy immensely, and return year after year. So you are relying on someone else's remarks. Whoever accused us of putting on an anti-Christian play is either ignorant or malicious – or both. This story takes place in Persia a few hundred years before the birth of Christianity. So how could Christianity possibly be maligned? This whole matter is absolutely absurd."

"But I heard you used the term *goyim*."

"*Goy* means nation in Hebrew. Even the Jews, the people of Israel are referred to as a *goy*... And, moreover, the entire story appears in what you call the Old Testament, which is part of your Bible. Surely you know the story of how Queen Esther saved the Jews from the evil Haman who wanted to kill all the Jews. So when we criticize Haman and his wife, Zeresh, we criticize those godless pagans who wanted to commit mass murder. Surely in our wonderful Italy where the Jews have lived since pre-Roman time in peace you do not side with Haman."

In my heart I applauded Papa Yossi for arguing so forcefully and so logically.

Like a fly he pinned Father Antonio to the wall. The priest

couldn't say a word. And I could see he didn't like the position he was in. Yossi cleverly appealed to his knowledge of the Bible and to his Italianness. Unless the priest was a thoroughgoing anti-Semite; if so, there was not much Papa could do.

Still, the priest surprised us.

"You are a carpenter?"

"A historic, noble occupation, just like...if you know what I mean."

The priest gave a wintry smile. He knew Yossi's hint at Jesus's line of work.

"I see indeed that you are a clever Jew, Giuseppe, and I will take what you have said under consideration. In the mean time I propose this: we will have a wordless public debate, you and I, with no words, but only sign language. It is an old, useful tested method of settling a dispute. We work with three signs. I offer one, you reply, and so on. Consider it a kind of play, like the one you put on recently. If you win, fine. The matter is closed. And if I win..."

"Yes? What if you win?" Papa Yossi said.

"Then I may have to pass this entire matter on to the Bishop."

"And continue this absurd accusation? I'm sure the Bishop knows the Bible."

The priest shrugged.

"And who will judge this debate?" Papa asked.

"I will."

"What? You initiate, you participate, and you will also judge?"

There came that soft, slippery, thin-lipped smile of winter again.

"Do you not trust me?" said the priest.

"How about if I decide," Yossi shot back.

"No, that won't work."

"Do you not trust me?"

At Papa Yossi's repetition of the priest's question, Antonio said:

"I know that our mayor, Giorgio Calmani, is your friend. Of course, I know him too. He will be invited. And I am sure that if he sees any injustice he will be first to speak up. We both know that he is a thoroughly secular man, not at all in favor of the church... Do you accept my invitation to participate?"

Yossi answered, "I will think it over."

"Give me your answer within three days, for I would like to schedule this debate for the middle of next week. If you do not wish to participate in this debate any other adult member of the Jewish community can do it. Even the rabbi."

Then the priest added: "The debate will take place in the church courtyard."

But clever Papa Yossi, surely knowing the priest would refuse, suggested the synagogue courtyard.

"Impossible. Out of the question," said the indignant Antonio.

"Then let's make it neutral territory," Yossi said. "How about the little square in front of the Municipal Library?"

To this the priest agreed.

Yossi told Antonio that he would give him his decision within three days. Then he and the priest bid each other goodbye without shaking hands. Antonio hardly looked at me and did not even ask Yossi who I was. I was dying to tell him that I had played Esther in the Purim-shpil, but since Yossi said nothing, I of course kept still.

But on our way home I did say: "I'm glad he's inviting the mayor."

"Yes. That's very good. I'm sure Giorgio's going to be there."

I remarked to Papa that the priest took no notice of me.

"Don't let it bother you. He was focused on something else."

"You spoke so eloquently, Papa."

"Truth and justice are aids to the tongue."

"But can you really trust him, Papa?"

"We have no choice. But since he said that my friend, the mayor, will be present, I think that's a good sign. And the fact that he suggested it on his own and not coming from me is also a good sign. You know what? Don't worry. I am confident it will go well."

Nevertheless, I felt uneasy. How could a simple woodworker, although smart and a good arguer, how could he compete with signs that will probably be connected to religion, how could he compete with the priest?

So I said: "I know you said no before, Papa, but still, maybe the rabbi, who knows religion better, maybe he should be the one to do this debate, this contest with the priest."

"No... no... no," Yossi said, like three beats on a bass drum. "We went through this before." He regarded me with a thoughtful and slightly anxious look on his face, then said:

"If this debate is weighted in favor of the priest and I lose, it is not an insult against our community if a simple woodworker is defeated. But if the rabbi, the head of the Jewish community, participates and loses, it is a blow against his prestige and honor – and a dark mark against all of us. So under no circumstances will I ask anyone else to do this debate. Antonio chose me as the founder of this Purim-shpil. He probably knows I started organizing this annual event years ago. No, this is going to be my affair. The priest threw a challenge my way and I will take him up on it."

Since I was so worried about Papa, I decided to speak to him and mention the mayor, even though he said he would like to do this on his own. "How about asking Giorgio to intervene, to persuade the priest to cancel this debate? After all, he's the mayor."

"Enough, Tinocchia. Under no circumstances will the priest cancel the debate. In this part of the country the church is very strong, even though few people are religious and observant. The good thing is that there will be an audience for the debate. If they see something wrong they'll speak out. And so will the mayor."

The next day Papa Yossi informed the priest that he would participate. But it would have to be the Thursday of the following week because he had to be in Rome for a few days.

The priest agreed and the debate was scheduled to take place on the chosen Thursday at 2 pm in the little square in front of the Municipal Library.

37
Why Snub-nosed Geppetto Accents Telling Truth

During one of my visits to Pinocchio's house, Geppetto told us a bit about his childhood:

"Pinocchio, I'm going to tell you something about lying. I don't think I ever told you this, but do you know why I keep telling you not to lie? There is something personal in this and I'll share it with you. When I was a little boy, my parents also told me, just like I keep telling you, to tell the truth, not to lie. But I had a problem. Every time I told the truth my nose got shorter. It got to the point that I almost had no nose at all and the boys on the street, knowing why this always happened to me, would yell out, 'Here comes the little Truth-teller. Here comes No-nose.'

"So I was sort of forced to lie once in a while just so I wouldn't look like a freak. But I didn't like it. I didn't like to lie. So the lies I told were little lies, very tiny little fibs that helped keep a nose on my face. For instance, if my mother would ask me if I ate up that piece of cake that she saved for my father, I wouldn't say I ate it all up. Because if I said that my nose would shrink. So to protect my ability to breathe normally, I would make up a little story and say I had a bite or two but the maid ate the rest. In fact, the boys used to pay me to lie. 'Hey, No-nose, tell us a lie, quick! I'll give you a penny.' And right away I came back with, 'You said, two.' I've just shared with you my quickest and shortest lie."

To which Pinocchio replied, and he threw me a quick glance, and what a fresh answer that was, "You just made all this up, Geppetto, to teach me about lying."

Short-nosed Geppetto just smiled.

But I suspected Pinocchio was right. Geppetto was using one big lie to persuade Pinocchio to stop fibbing.

I considered for a moment what I was going to say, and then said it:

Curt Leviant

"Geppetto, I hope you don't mind if I quote our greatest poet, Dante, who said something significant about lying."

To which Pinocchio muttered, "Show off!"

"No, Tinocchia, go right ahead. Especially if it's Dante."

"Dante said, '*La poesia e una...*"

"...*bella menzogna*,'" Pinocchio finished for me. "Poetry is a beautiful lie."

Geppetto looked at Pinocchio with surprise. So did I.

"I heard it before from her," Pinocchio said, pointing at me.

"And you remembered," I said. "That's pretty good. I'm impressed."

By the twinkle in Pinocchio's eyes I knew something rascally was coming. And I was right. Then that little devil of a puppetto added:

"And if you reverse that saying it's still beautiful and correct: A beautiful lie is poetry. Sheer poetry."

38
Stray Thoughts Before Falling Asleep

At night before I fell asleep stray thoughts floated through my head, like wind-blown leaves falling from trees in late October. I thought of Table rolling on its own. Then Yossi at his worktable with a nail in his mouth ready to hammer it in. And the swan at the water's edge, the birds tweeting in the forest at dusk. The crickets at night had a special rhythmic song of their own, chittering that started on the left side of the trees, climbed up, and descended on the right. It was like an invisible rainbow of sound. For a moment I saw, then quickly blinked her away – Zeresh. And then the upcoming debate with the priest insinuated itself. I turned in the bed to chase it away. I thought of the birds again. Of sunshine. I felt the warmth of the day, the roses in our garden. Little pieces of conversation I had with Pinocchio ran through my mind. I recalled without even wanting to what he said about not lying any more. "I'll change. I'll turn myself inside out. Upside down. I'll tell so many truths my nose will disappear."

"No. I've always loved your nose. That's what makes you, you."

"All right. It'll be hard but I'll try to lie once in a while," he said.

And then I reheard him telling me his name was Nipocchio and Geppetto scolded him and I felt myself smiling at that and I saw the falling leaves suspended in mid-air and I couldn't hold on to my thoughts anymore and everything slowed down and I fell asleep.

39
Duplicate "Tua." Tinocchia's Trick

Two days later Papa Yossi surprised me. He looked so delighted it almost seemed he had forgotten about the debate with the priest the following week.

"Come into my workshop."

I followed him in, looked at the far side of the shop, and became confused.

If I was over here, what was I doing over there?

Or was it a mirror Yossi had put on the other side of the room? Ever since I learned about mirrors, I thought I had mastered the art of mirror looking.

But then my image in the looking glass, the girl who looked just like me, moved.

"What's...who's that?"

Yossi's face lit up. "I always wanted twins." He looked at me and smiled. "But don't worry. She's just temporary. Remember, I have to go to Rome for a few days and I don't want you to be alone. I made her from a few pieces of scattered wood for you to have some company while I'm away. She can't talk but she understands everything and she will listen to whatever you tell her. You can play games with her and read a book to her. But just don't go far from the house. Remember what happened with the swan by the river?"

"Yes, Papa. I know... But why can't she talk?"

Yossi gave me an ambiguous answer. "Because that's the way she was made."

I reflected on the way I was made with the ability to talk and silently thanked Yossi for this.

"Does she have a name?"

"Not yet. If you wish you can name her."

"Hmm," I mumbled, looking at my twin. "Fine. Since she looks so much like me and she's your puppetta, I'll call her Tua." And then I spoke to her:

"Your name is Tua. It means 'your' in Italian."

Then Yossi stood in front of her and, pointing to me, said:

"Tua. This is Tinocchia. She's going to be your sister for a while. Whatever she tells you to do you will do. Do you understand?"

Tua nodded.

"I'll come back to you later," I told my twin.

Then I had an idea. "Papa, I'm going to go to Geppetto's house for a minute. I'll be right back."

But Pinocchio wasn't home, so I asked Geppetto, "Please tell Pinocchio to come see me later in the afternoon."

In the hallway I stood before the mirror, not because of vanity, just reflection. In both senses of the word. I looked at myself, in myself. Picturing the other image of me who could not talk that Yossi had just made, I probed more deeply into what made me, me. I closed my eyes and saw Tinocchia through closed eyes, a small picture of myself at the top of my head, somewhere behind my eyelids. Can you imagine? Imagination can see without eyesight.

Ever since I discovered the looking-glass it has fascinated me. When I first looked into the glass, I was frightened at seeing someone else. Then I realized it was me. Still, it was endlessly amazing. Someone right next to me; well, opposite me, who looked like me, moved and imitated my movements. She flaps her arms, grimaces, but can't talk. But I was the master of this imitation me. I was the one who initiated; it followed. It could not do anything first and make me follow. After all, we're not in a world of make-believe. Nor in any magic mirror that Yossi creates. Wouldn't it be strange if my image in the mirror would begin to talk?

Looking at myself in the mirror I thought of the me-ness of me. There is only one me, even though another puppetta looks quite like me. I am the only me in the world – nobody else is me. Not even Tua, who looks like me. Not even the me in the glass who disappears when I move away. But I don't disappear when I slide from the mirror. If that me in the mirror isn't me, that image that looks exactly like me, then surely no one else can be me.

Except me.

So the question can someone else be me is meaningless.

And what is the me-ness of me, anyway? When I sleep, does the me in me go away, or does it just sleep too, and when I wake – zhoop!, it flies instantly back into me?

Or is it suspended outside of me when my eyes are closed, hovering like a butterfly near me, waiting for me to wake? Or does it remain within me even when I sleep? And if it does hover suspended outside of me when I sleep, how can I be sure that if flies back into *me* when I wake and not into someone else, like, for instance, Tua? But that, it seems, would go against nature. So probably one's me-ness never departs, day or night.

And is this me-ness transferable? If I concentrate, can I put my me-ness into another person? Like Tua? Probably not. And you know what? I wouldn't even want to try.

And what about other people's views of me? Is that too considered part of my me-ness? And does one add up my views of myself with others' views, and that is the totality of a person?

Considering this, being able to think about my me-ness, I realized I was not a mere puppetta, a dummy – actually, a marionette, although no one pulls *my* strings. If I could think of this me, the like of which exists nowhere else in the world, then I am beyond puppet-tree. I'm not quite like Yossi or Geppetto, but inside me, within me, I feel like them and all the other people who walk the streets.

Soon as I heard Pinocchio's knock on the door I yelled out, "Just a minute," and I told my double to stand facing me, about four feet away.

"A boy named Pinocchio will come in," I told Tua. "He's a puppetto like you and me. When he comes into the room you imitate

Curt Leviant

exactly what I do. When I raise my hands, you raise your hands at the exact same time. Just like in a mirror." But then I realized she has probably never seen a mirror, so I added, "Let's practise... Fine ... But when I tell him to shut his eyes for a moment and then open them, we will do something different. At that time, do *not* imitate me. For instance, if I raise my hand, you raise your foot. Do anything except what I do. And sometimes don't even move. Do you understand?"

Tua nodded.

Then I told Pinocchio to come in and stand in the doorway. I stood in the middle of the room. Tua opposite me. Pinocchio shifted his gaze between me and my double a few times.

"Who's that? What's going on? Come on, Tinocchia, say something."

"All right. I'll tell you. My father made a magic mirror for me. He has been doing that recently. You haven't seen that magic pin-hole mirror he created... No, no, don't move. Stay where you are. You can't come near. Just watch from where you are. If you come closer the magic disappears...Now watch."

I lifted my hands. Tua too. I bent sideways. So did she. I stretched my hands over my head. I flapped my arms as if they were wings. Tua mirrored all my motions.

"Now close your eyes, Pinocchio. When I tell you to open them again you will see the magic mirror doing wonders."

I sent a little warning signal to Tua; again, she nodded.

"All right, open your eyes."

I raised my right hand. Tua did nothing. I bent forward. Tua spun around. I held my head. She bent down. I applauded. Tua shook her head from side to side.

"What's going on?" Pinocchio cried. "What kind of mirror is that?"

"I told you it's a magic mirror. Step forward a bit and make faces. See if the mirror answers."

But as much as Pinocchio tried, he saw nothing.

"The magic mirror doesn't work for you," I said, teasing him.

Then I took Tua by the hand and we danced quickly around Pinocchio. When I was behind him for a moment I told him to point to the real Tinocchia once we had stopped dancing.

Tua and I stood side by side.

Pinocchio looked at me and then at Tua. He stood there, not moving. The only thing that moved on him were his two big brown eyes, staring, unblinking from one puppetta to the other.

"What's this? Who made this mirror image?" Pinocchio put his hands on his hips. "Come on, say something."

But I remained silent.

Pinocchio pressed a finger to his cheek. "Let's see. Only one of you is real. The other is a duplicate. One is the real Tinocchia, the other, false, skillfully made to look like you."

He stared intently at both of us; then Pinocchio pointed to me.

"You are the true, the real, Tinocchia."

"How can you tell?" I asked.

"A breath of living spirit," he said. "I sensed it in the sparkle of your eyes." Then he looked at Tua. She lowered her gaze. "Head and hands and hair – the three h's – can be imitated. But the life sparkle in the eyes, never."

Insulted, my twin spun about and ran off to the workshop in a huff – so quickly she left a wave of cold wind behind her. Tua, I thought, she's got something of me in her, turning around and showing her back when she's upset.

"The mirror is gone," I said.

"What kind of trick is that? I've never seen anything like this before."

"My Papa Yossi made her to keep me company for a few days while he's out of town."

Then I ran into the workshop. Tua was sitting on Yossi's workbench, her head lowered, her fists supporting her cheeks. I went up to her, put my arm around her shoulder and pressed her close.

"Don't mind him, Tua. He just babbles," I said softly. "You played that mirror game beautifully. As if we've been rehearsing for years."

And I kissed her cheek. Had someone put a mirror in front of us I wouldn't have been able to tell who was Tinocchia and who was Tua.

I don't want to exaggerate, but it seemed to me that after this affectionate embrace and my kind words and my kiss on her cheek, I think I saw the tiniest glisten, almost a teardrop, in each of her eyes.

And I felt sorry that Papa had created her only temporarily. And then I put my feeling into action and when he came back I persuaded him to let her live on as a new puppetta.

But the make-believe mirror really wasn't gone. Later, it played a role in, and was the cause of, a dispute.

40
Tinocchia Jealous of Image in Mirror

A day or so afterwards, at my house, Pinocchio picked up a round, hand-held mirror with a bright brown orange wooden frame. He stood next to me, stretched out his hand, and held it so that he saw my face.

Then I saw him taking this mirror, evidently wanting to keep my image, which stayed in the glass for a few minutes after I had stopped looking into it. This was another of Yossi's mirror inventions, which I cannot explain.

But a while later I saw him furtively looking at the glass. Perhaps now, I thought, there's an image there of another girl.

"You have another girl friend," I said. "Zeresh."

"Anyone who slaps my face can't be my girl friend."

"But that was only in the Purim-shpil."

"Still."

"Then it's another girl friend."

"What do you mean another girl friend? I don't even have one."

That hurt.

"All right," I said. "We'll go to the rabbino and he'll decide who's right."

"Why do we have to bring him in?"

"Because he's a good impartial judge."

"But he's a Jew like you. He'll side with you."

"You don't know our Rabbino dei Rossi. He is a just and honest man. Davide dei Rossi, who has been rabbi in Siena for more than thirty years, stems from one of Italy's oldest Jewish families, who trace their ancestry in Italy back to pre-Roman times."

At the rabbi's house I was tempted to – I was yearning to – tell him about next week's debate between Papa Yossi and Father Antonio. But remembering what Papa said I kept still.

"Shalom," he said. "Welcome. "What can I do for you?"

"It's a mirror problem and we'd like you to solve it for us... Pinocchio keeps looking at the image of his girlfriend in this glass. It's the wicked Zeresh."

"She's pretty wicked," Pinocchio said and laughed, "which means she's wicked and pretty."

"I know you played Haman, but I see your neck hasn't been separated from the rest of your body," the rabbino joked with Pinocchio.

But at this Pinocchio did not even smile.

"Let me see that glass," the rabbi said. He took it and looked into it. He stretched his hand out, gazed at the mirror from an arm's length, then held it close to his face. Then he turned the glass upside down. He grimaced, smiled, frowned.

"What's all the fuss about?" said Rabbino dei Rossi. "The only person in this glass is me."

And while he was holding it, he invited us to stand in back of him and look into the looking-glass to see who we could see.

*One day, during the summer, when I had no classes, I was bored, which never happened to me before, because I always had a book to read. I had finished one book of old Italian stories and had not yet begun a new one. And I didn't watch Yossi doing his woodwork. And I didn't want to see Pinocchio because it seemed to me he was interested in Zeresh. Once, in the market, I thought I saw the two of them bidding goodbye to each other, but I must confess the sun was in my eyes so maybe suspicion distorted my vision.

And I was dying to go out on an adventure, but if I would depart for a few hours Yossi would worry. Luckily, without knowing it, Yossi came to my aid.

He said, "Tinocchia, I'm going to Milan for a few days. I heard there is a supply of a marvelous wood from Brazil. Do you want to come with me?"

"No, Papa, thank you. I'd rather not go."

"Well, by now you're old enough to be on your own." And then, with a twinkle in his eye, a twinkle that went all the way down to his mustache, he added: "And of course, if you went with me, that would be several days without Pinocchio."

"Well," I said with a faint smile, but I said no more. I didn't want to tell him about the problems I'd been having with that rascally puppetto.

-- -

*I found this loose page in the mss. Since it pertains to Tinocchia's suspicion of Pinocchio liking Zeresh, I have included it here. The author evidently did not pursue an expansion of this page with any other chapter, but since this passage is revelatory of Tinocchia's feelings, I felt that the reader should see it. Another discrepancy here is Yossi's trip to Milan. He had just gone to Rome a few pages earlier. Ed.]

Curt Leviant

41

Tinocchia Meditates on Letters of Her Name

Years ago, Papa Yossi told me that when I would be older and had a better understanding of Hebrew, he would explain some fascinating things about my Hebrew name. And this is what he told me the other day.

Although my name, Tinocchia, sounds quite Italian, just like Pinocchio's, the basic root of my name, which I mentioned earlier, comes from the Hebrew word for baby, *tinok*. However, examined more closely, it's a bit more complicated and sophisticated. For instance, my name can be divided into two Hebrew words: *Tinok ya* (*ya* is one of the short names of God, like in the popular word, hal-lelu-ya, praise God). In that form my name can mean baby of God. Not, heaven forbid, that God made that child, but in the sense that the baby was sort of a divine gift.

When I was eleven or twelve Papa Yossi told me to hold my hands up and out and stand with my legs about two feet apart. When I did this, he asked me, "Which letter of the Hebrew alphabet do you look like now?

"The aleph," I said at once.

Yossi smiled. "You see, when I formed you, that was your shape on my table, just before the living breath went into you. So you have within you the *aleph*, the first letter of the Hebrew alphabet, or the A, the first letter of the Italian alphabet, and also the *tav*, the last letter of the Hebrew alphabet. So the *aleph* or A and the *tav* are part of your name, in inverse fashion. The last letter of the Hebrew alphabet is the first letter of your name, Tinocchia... are you follow-ing?"

"Yes, Papa," I said, although it was a bit complicated.

"And when your name is spelled in Italian, the A, the first letter of the Italian alphabet, is the last letter of your name."

"That is so nice and balanced," I said.

"And so, because of the way you were shaped, I always think of you as an aleph. Years ago, when you were younger, I told you you were too young to understand the mystical aspects connected to your name. But now that you have studied and learned you'll be able to appreciate it... Now listen, what's the opening verse of the Torah?"

I recited it in Hebrew, then translated it: "In beginning God created heaven and earth."

"How many words?"

"Seven."

"In which words do *alephs* appear?" my father asked.

I envisioned the words, as if they were on a placard before me.

"An *aleph* appears in every word but one, the word *shamayim*, which means 'heaven.'"

"Right," said Yossi. "And from a kabbalistic or mystical point of view one might say that the *aleph* is earthbound, like the six days of work we observe, but not the seventh word, the one for 'heaven', which is above and beyond us, but we try to imitate heaven on earth by resting on the seventh day. Now you remember that the *aleph*, the first letter of the Hebrew alphabet and the *tav*, the last letter, are bound to your name. So from a kabbalistic reading one can say that God created you."

"How is that? I thought you made me, Papa?"

"I mean, inspired by the One Above. The first three words of the Torah mean, 'In the beginning God created.' Created what? What's the next word in Hebrew? How is it spelled."

I replied, "The next word is a short one, *et*, composed of just two letters, the *aleph* and the *tav*. Or A and T."

"Right," Yossi said. "What did God create? *Et.* That word with those two letters with which your name is linked. So that verse that opens the Bible can be read as: In the beginning God created that girl whose initials are *aleph* and *tav*... You!"

I was so amazed at this a shiver of fright and awe ran through me. Papa Yossi noticed this and put his arms around me and kissed me.

"Nothing to be frightened of, darling girl. I'm just playing with the letters of your name."

"Your reading of the Torah verse seems rather far-fetched, Papa."

"Well, perhaps. But in Judaism names are very important, and yours is a very rich and meaningful one."

But I have a hunch that Papa did all this to somehow tie his very human, hand-made creation to the real Creator and justify his *imitatio dei*.

42
The Mistress of Feelings

And while I was thinking these lofty thoughts about Hebrew letters and their mystical connections, other thoughts – turmoil – were churning within me. I either said aloud these words or saw them spelled out before my eyes.

"She was no longer mistress of her own feelings."

I had read that line in the love story, "The Novel of Juliet", by our own 16th century writer, Luigi da Porta. Yes, that very same doomed Romeo and Juliet romance Shakespeare used a few decades later for his famous tragedy.

In this story Juliet says the line I just quoted, and her sensations echoed in me when I thought of that rascal, Pinocchio. Yes, those last two words are wedded to each other.

In truth, no longer was I mistress of my feelings. I tried to rein in my affection for this simple puppetto, but Pinocchio reigned over me. He was now the master of my emotions, and I – mistress of none. But there the comparison between Pinocchio and me and the fictional Romeo and Juliet ended.

For our fathers, Geppetto and Yossi, as you know by now, were not blood enemies but best of friends. So, thinking of Pinocchio, I recalled Luigi da Porta's oddly formal yet heartfelt words about a girl's inner turmoil in love. A girl who realizes she could no longer control her own emotions.

Oh, my! I was thinking of myself and forgetting about Papa and the burden placed upon him by the priest. The day of the debate was approaching.

43
The Signs Debate of Yossi and the Priest

Benches were placed in the little park in front of the municipal library. Yossi and Father Antonio stood there before a crowd of about fifty people. Most were seated on the benches; some sat on the ground, chatting and laughing. There was a pleasant picnic mood in the air.

The priest welcomed everyone to the signs debate. He did not give reasons for the wordless exchange but said it would be between him and the carpenter Giuseppe, representing the Jewish community.

"This is how the wordless debate will proceed. I will make a sign without speaking and carpenter Giuseppe will respond without saying a word. Do you agree, Giuseppe?"

Yossi nodded.

"Say Yes or No."

Yossi smartly pointed to his tongue, and wagged his finger, as if reminding the priest that this was, per his condition, a wordless debate. I looked about and saw everyone smiling.

"You are permitted to say Yes or No."

"I thought I am not allowed to speak."

"You can for this reply. I just want everyone assembled here to know that you understand and agree that this debate, once it is started, is only with gestures and no talking is permitted. As I said, there will be three signs to which you will respond. Do you agree and understand?"

"Yes," Yossi replied, hesitated a moment, then said, "Do you?"

The surprised priest at once said, "Yes, I too agree."

I was so proud of my smart Papa. Anyone smart enough to create a talking puppetta like me had to be smart enough to answer a priest's sign language.

I sat in the first row. Sitting there too was Yossi's friend, Giorgio, the Mayor of Siena. And when I turned a moment later, I was surprised to see Geppetto and Pinocchio a few rows behind me. I waved to them and they smiled and waved back. I also saw that quite a number of Jews from the community had come to cheer Yossi on. I did not see Zeresh. No doubt she did not dare to show her face here.

By now Rabbino dei Rossi knew about the debate. Papa Yossi decided to tell him, for he felt the rabbi would surely get news of it and it would have been disrespectful not to inform him in advance. The rabbi wished Yossi well and said that although he would have liked to see how Yossi responded to the signs, he would not dignify this church-sponsored event with his presence. Yossi told the rabbi he fully agreed. He never even thought of asking him to come.

Now the priest clanged a little bell and put his finger to his lips. The crowd fell silent.

For the first sign Antonio pulled out of his pocket a wooden matchstick. He bent down, scratched it on a cobblestone until it burst into flame. He held up the burning matchstick and shook it toward Yossi.

I wondered what Papa would do in reply.

The faces in the crowd turned now from the priest to Yossi, who stood about ten feet away from him. I too looked at Papa, quietly praying for his success.

But Yossi seemed baffled. He stared at the priest's hand holding the burning match. Then he turned and looked at me for a moment. Was he perhaps wanting help? Suddenly, I had an idea. I lifted my right fist to my mouth very gradually and tilted my head backward slightly. At once Papa got the hint.

He took from his pocket the little jug of water he had prepared in case he got thirsty. He removed the cork and, as he stretched out his hand and jiggled it toward the priest, he poured the water on the cobblestones as though he were pouring the water on the priest's feet.

Of course, the priest did not say a word.

But I think I saw a fleeting expression of dismay on Antonio's face.

Again the priest lifted his little bell.

But since the crowd was quiet, he did not ring it.

For his second sign the priest took from his jacket a piece of glass about four by five centimeters and looked through it. I sensed at once what Papa would do, for he always carried it with him. He showed his pin-hole mirror, flashed it once in the rays of the sun, looked at himself, and then put it to his eyes, looking through it at the priest.

Again I closely watched the priest's reaction; a slight downward turn of his thin bluish lips.

For the third sign, Antonio held up his index finger and waved it at Yossi. My father took a deep breath, then held up two fingers and waved them toward the priest.

The priest's eyes opened wide and he shook his head, as if in disbelief. Then that wan, weak smile came over his face and he addressed the crowd:

"The Jewish carpenter Giuseppe has answered all my signs excellently. I did not think that this could be accomplished. I did not believe that anyone could do it." Then Antonio turned to my father and said, "But you did."

The audience applauded. The mayor stood and applauded Papa Yossi. Seeing this, everyone sitting on the benches and on the ground stood and clapped hands in honor of my father, who was smiling and thanking the crowd, both hands on his heart.

And then, to our astonishment, the priest came over and shook Yossi's hand. The mayor came to Papa and embraced him. So did I. Geppetto approached and hugged his old friend and kissed him on both cheeks. And Pinocchio shook my hand and Yossi's. And now, since everyone was kissing, the rascal came back to me and kissed my cheek.

The people in the audience gathered around my father and

congratulated him. The priest withdrew, the skirts of his long black robe moving quickly with the speed of his departure. And then, nodding and waving to everyone, Yossi and I made our way home.

But first we stopped in at Rabbino dei Rossi's house to report to him. He welcomed us warmly. "Well?" he said in an upbeat tone, as if anticipating good news. "I see you're smiling."

"You were right, rabbi. After the debate the priest announced that I had answered all the signs excellently. He said he thought it couldn't be done but that I did. And he even came over to me and shook my hand."

"Quite astounding that the priest admitted publicly that you had bested him. Well, this is still Italy and not Torquemada's Spain. It's a different type of Catholicism here with a different type of population. Mazal tov."

"Thank you. And the audience clapped."

"I'm not surprised. The Sienese are good people. How many came?"

"You know, rabbi, I was so intent on answering the signs I did not even look at the audience." Then Papa looked at me, indicating that I should answer.

"I'd say between fifty and sixty. Most on benches, some on the ground. And quite a number from our community. There was a festive atmosphere all around. Just like at the Purim-shpil."

"Which, as you know, I was unable to attend," the rabbino said. "This is the first Purim-shpil I have ever missed. Tell me, Yossi, even though I prefer words to gestures, I'd like to know what the priest's signs were and how you responded. This signs debate must have been very hard for you. After all, no words."

"Actually, rabbi, no. I thought it was quite easy. Well, let's say it went very well after the first sign. For the first one Antonio struck a matchstick on the cobblestones and held up the burning match. That puzzled me for a moment – until Tinocchia came to my aid."

"How is that?" the rabbi asked.

"I looked at her for a moment and it almost seemed without

moving my smart little girl brought her hand to her mouth and mimed drinking water. That gave me the answer. By the way, Tinocchia, how did you think of this?"

"Well, Papa, soon as I saw the flame I immediately thought of a line in the song, *Chad Gadya*, that we sing at the end of the Seder, where the water douses the fire. So when you looked at me I made the sign for drinking and you understood the rest."

"Yes, Tinocchia, wonderful. And then I understood that by lighting a match and pointing it to me Antonio seemed to be telling me that if he wished he could burn my workshop. I'm always afraid of fire. Fire is my greatest fear. So I have pails of water always prepared. But I also had with me my little jug of water in case I got thirsty. So, after Tinocchia's hint, actually her wordless sign, in response to his fire I took out my water. I opened the little jug and poured it on the ground toward him, signaling that I am always prepared to fight fire with water."

"Bravo!" cried the rabbi. "Wonderful. And the second sign?"

"For the second sign the priest took out a clear piece of glass and looked through it, as if to say, I can watch you through my window. I answered him this way. From my pocket I took out this mirror, which I created with tiny pinholes and I flashed it in the sunlight to show him my glass was silvered while his was plain. I showed him that with this glass I could see him and myself, while with his glass he could only see me."

The rabbi nodded and said, "Good. Good. And the third sign?"

"By the displeased expression on the priest's face after my first two answers it seemed to me that I was answering correctly. So when he put out one finger and pointed it at me, hinting that he could poke out one of my eyes, I didn't hesitate but right away put up two fingers and jabbed them toward him to say that if he tried that I would take out both of his eyes."

"Looks like you really showed him. Quick thinking, Yossi."

"And in doing this I learned something."

"What?" the rabbino asked.

"That we can get along without words. Just like I do all day long working by myself."

"But we need words, Yossi. We cannot get along just with signs and symbols. Speaking is what distinguishes us from the animals."

Soon as I said that a thought ran through my mind: I'm glad I can speak. Otherwise, I'd have been insulted.

And as if the rabbi read my mind, he added:

"It's only because you constantly spoke to Tinocchia that she learned and began to speak."

"You're right, rabbi. We do need words."

Rabbino dei Rossi smiled. "Imagine conducting prayers to God with just signs."

"The synagogue would be a very quiet place," I said, and both men laughed.

"But you know," Yossi said, "I remember my grandfather, who came here from Poland because of persecutions of Hasidim in Vilna, telling me about a Hasidic story he heard about a little uneducated boy who came from a farming village. He was a simple country boy, about ten years old, and could not read Hebrew. He came to pray in a synagogue. He stood there silently in the back and then, suddenly, whistled. All the men berated him for being a boor. One does not whistle in the synagogue. Peasants, cowherds, whistle. Not Jews. But the rabbi defended him, saying, 'His prayer is accepted above yours because he prayed from the heart.'"

"Thank you, Yossi, for this. I have never heard this story before. So you see, sometimes signs are useful. Sometimes God answers with signs. We use words and He answers with signs. We pray for rain with words and he responds without words and sends the sign—rain. In any case, I'm so proud of you, Yossi," the rabbi said. "It was very courageous of you to accept the challenge."

I noticed that the rabbi did not say "the priest's challenge." He didn't like to use the word "priest" too often.

"Well, I didn't like the idea that someone had maliciously told Antonio about an anti-Christian element in the Purim-shpil. When I met the priest, I had to summarize the meglla story for him, which he probably never read..."

"You're right. Never. Believe me, they never look at our book which they call the Old Testament."

Then we said goodbye to the rabbino and went home.

It wasn't until much later that we learned how different was the priest's interpretation of his own and of Yossi's signs.

We now were busy with making preparations for the holiday of Passover which was soon coming. It was during that beautiful Festival of Freedom that I learned something about doing a good deed and its occasional rough edges, for during both Seder nights unusual incidents occurred that we will never forget.

44
At the Seder

The beautiful Spring holiday of Passover.

For the Seder Yossi placed on the festive table his mother's silver candlesticks, his hand-embossed silver Kiddush cup, and the big silver Cup of Elijah, both of which came from his grandfather. The matza he had ordered from the matza bakery in Florence was delivered to the Siena railroad station where he picked it up. After setting the table for the Seder, at sundown we went to the synagogue for the Evening Service. After prayers all the congregants wished one another "chag same'akh". As we were about to leave, we saw a stranger lingering by the front door.

"Are you visiting here?" Papa Yossi asked him. "Waiting for someone you know?"

"No, I know no one here. I'm from Naples. I had to make my way north to Venice but I could not do it in time so I had to remain here in Siena. Is there a hotel where I can stay?"

"I mean, isn't it rather late to look for a hotel after prayers on the first night of Passover?"

"It's too complicated to go into. You see, I'm sort of stuck here."

"Well, there's no hotel in the area."

Seeing that the man was crestfallen Yossi said at once, "But don't worry. I'm inviting you to my house for the Seder. And you can spend the first two days of the holiday with us."

"That is so kind of you, but..."

"But what? How can we leave a fellow Jew alone with nowhere to go on Pesach... What's your name?

"My name is Shalom, and I thank you from the bottom of my heart for your Jewish hospitality. I hope I am not a burden."

"It's all right. We have room for you. Tonight we have no guests, but we will have some tomorrow. There is plenty for everyone and it will be a great joy for us."

The man ticked his head and clucked with his tongue. "What a mitzva! What a generous deed!"

The man's Italian was a bit atilt, as though he wasn't proficient in it. Or it may have been a dialect from down South; however, we were able to understand each other.

At home I lit the candles for the holiday and, at the Seder, Yossi made Kiddush over the wine. As is customary, Papa asked Shalom if he too would like to chant Kiddush but he politely declined. I sang the *Ma Nishtana*, the Four Questions, in Hebrew and Italian, which the guest praised, perhaps more than was necessary. We continued reciting the Hagada, singing all the traditional songs as we did every year. But I found it strange that our guest, Shalom, either did not know the melodies or did not want to sing with us.

Then, at the point in the Seder when it came to opening the door to welcome Elijah the Prophet, an amazing thing happened. Since the youngest always does this, I went to the door. Usually, no one is there. But when I opened it, to my astonishment, a man with a long grey beard stood before me. He was nicely dressed and wore an old-fashioned cap.

"I bring you greetings from Jerusalem," he said in Hebrew.

Excitedly, I ran back to Yossi and Shalom.

"There's an old man with a long beard standing in the doorway and he said in Hebrew, I bring you greetings from Jerusalem."

"Why didn't you invite him in?" Yossi asked.

"I was so excited I wanted to tell you first."

"Go back and invite him in."

But Yossi didn't wait for me. He ran to the door. By the time he opened it he saw that the visitor was no longer there.

"He's gone," Yossi said sadly.

"Don't be upset," Shalom said. "You are very fortunate. That was surely Elijah." Then he turned to me. "Did you ask him for anything?"

"No. Why should I ask a stranger who appears at our door for anything? Usually, it's a stranger who asks."

"Well, when this happens at the Seder night, and it doesn't happen often, I have heard that people make requests. At least that's our tradition in southern Italy. Fortunately, we have two Seders. Maybe he will come tomorrow night again. I certainly hope he does. If he does and he says he brings greetings from Jerusalem, very likely it's Elijah, and we should ask him for some kind of blessing."

The next morning we went to the synagogue. At lunch Shalom wasn't very talkative. I wanted to ask him about life in southern Italy and what he did. Papa asked him a few questions about where he was born and what kind of education he got, but his answers weren't very clear. It almost felt he was speaking another language. And after lunch he said he would take a walk into town. Siena was so pretty and inviting, he said, especially the old main square.

For the second Seder Yossi had invited another couple and an elderly man. We told them about last night's experience and waited anxiously to see if the man we thought was Elijah would come again. When it came to opening the door—this time Papa Yossi and Shalom joined me—sure enough there again stood the old, grey-bearded man, smiling at us. Yossi offered him the Cup of Elijah, filled with wine, but the man now answered in Italian, not Hebrew:

"I have many houses to visit and many miles to go, so I can't drink from my cup."

Then Shalom spoke. "Excuse me for interrupting, Elijah, I'm only a guest here, but can my host..."—and here he pointed to Papa—"make use of the custom we have down south to ask Elijah for something."

"Of course. Go ahead..."

Elijah looked at us, waiting. But no one spoke. In awe of him there was silence. Then he addressed Yossi:

"Please. Do so. Don't be shy."

Yossi looked at Shalom and at Elijah.

Elijah nodded.

"Elijah, if you don't mind," Yossi said, "I would like to ask you, for it isn't every day that a house is privileged to have a visitor like you, the herald of the Messianic Age we have long been praying for and dreaming of. So we would like to ask for *shalom*, for peace, for the people of Israel and for the world. Also, can you, would you, give us something to remember you by, so that we can say that you were here?"

"Good. Fine. Yours is a very modest request. I will give you something even better."

And Elijah the Prophet took from his pocket a beautifully decorated beige silk handkerchief. A sweet perfume floated out of it.

"Sniff this sweet handkerchief, all of you at once, and make a wish. A wish that will come true. And this magic kerchief will be yours to keep."

Yossi and all the guests, including me, approached Elijah.

Then Elijah said to Shalom: "You, *signore*, over there. Why did you back away, if you were the one who spoke of a special request? Don't you want to have a wish?"

"I'm sorry, I have to explain. I would like to but I can't. Perfume makes me ill."

Elijah shrugged. "It's up to you. To get a wish one must sniff."

Elijah the Prophet beckoned all of us to come closer. He stretched out his hand with the handkerchief. All of us bent forward. As soon as they all took a deep whiff their heads made little circles and they slowly crumpled down to the floor. I too fell down, at least pretended to, because that potent potion that affected everyone else could not affect me.

I lay with my head on my elbow and managed to keep one eye partially open to see what was happening.

"Hurry," Elijah called out, evidently to Shalom. "This perfume lasts only about ten minutes. Let's get moving."

And I saw Elijah take a pillow case from his pocket. He and

our Seder guest, Shalom, snuffed out the little flames in the candles and snatched Yossi's silver candlesticks and all the silverware and put them into the pillowcase. Elijah poured some of the wine from the Cup of Elijah into Papa's Kiddush cup. The two men clinked cups. They sang out, "L'Chaim!" and drank up the wine. Then they threw both silver cups into the pillow case.

I was about to jump up, surprise them, and shout, "Stop, thieves!" but I was afraid that with the two big men against me I did not have a chance. Who knows what violence these thieves were capable of?

So I waited.

When they left, I was sure they were headed. Downhill. Out of town.

And I knew exactly what to do.

"Table!" I called.

Table rolled toward me.

"We're going for a ride."

I picked Table up, set it outside on the street and sat down in the sitting box.

"Let's go after the crooks. One at a time."

Rolling down we went faster and faster. The two men were running, unaware that on this warm spring night something was rumbling behind them.

I aimed Table toward Elijah carrying the pillow case. Before he knew it Table had hit him in back of the knees and he went sprawling, screaming, knocking his head against the pavement. Then I aimed Table toward our guest who was running even quicker, not even turning to look back. And down he went too, rolling on the street, crying out in pain.

All the noise brought people out of their homes.

"Get them," I shouted. "They took all of Yossi's silverware, those thieves."

Soon two men came out of with ropes and bound both men. I took the white pillow case with the silver. Then I thanked Table for his good work and asked it, "Can you go up hill too?"

I had never done that before with Table.

He said, "Sure," and I sat on Table and up the hill we went.

In the house Papa and his guests were by now sitting on the floor, a bit dazed but feeling better.

I told them what I had done.

Yossi shook his head. "Jewish thieves," he said with a sad downspin to his voice. "On the night of the Seder. How well they planned it, those clever bandits! But we can't let them ruin our Seder. Come, let's continue."

And guess what I later found at the corner of Table? The eagle feather Pinocchio had given me that, he assured me, had magical powers. The feather I had disdainfully cast into the edge of the sitting box.

The next day I was a heroine in the synagogue and in town, and Rabbino dei Rossi thanked me during his sermon for my courage, imagination and initiative.

Nevertheless, all of us were downcast that the Elijah we expect for the Seder had not really come. And that a false Elijah had stolen not our silver but our golden hopes.

But even after all this Passover excitement we got some fascinating news.

We learned all about it when Papa Yossi's friend, Giorgio, the Mayor of Siena, dropped in to see us and told us some surprising details about the recent silent signs debate.

But before that we had another interesting experience.

45
The Palio Adventure

Sometimes the best adventure is the least expected one.

One afternoon we were in the center of Siena, Pinocchio and I, watching the famous Palio di Siena horse race, that annual festive event* where from each local district a horse and rider compete in a race around the Campo. Although people plan for this event all year long, believe it or not, the race lasts only about ninety seconds.

Soon as the horses began their dash Pinocchio suddenly said that he'd quickly run across to the other side of the track before the horses came. I told him not to dare. "You'll get killed, Pinocchio. Trampled."

"If your table couldn't hurt me when you bumped into me no horse will."

As Pinocchio was about to dart a stranger grabbed him with two hands and held his waist just as two horses unexpectedly speeded up and rushed by us with a burst of wind. In fact, one of the jockeys was thrown off and was caught by the crowd, something that happened every year* – for the jockeys ride bareback.

No doubt about it, this man saved Pinocchio's life.

"You're crazy," he shouted at the puppetto while still holding him.

But Pinocchio, breathing heavily, just said, "I could have done it."

"At least thank the man, Pinocchio," I said.

"You can call me Ambrosio," he said.

I looked at the man who had just saved that impetuous puppetto. He wore a cap and, though it was warm, a long-sleeved shirt. But what was most odd was that he had a strange, impassive,

-- --

*The Palio is actually run twice a year; the author either forgot this or did not want to confuse his readers by going into details. [Ed.]

almost immobile face.

"Don't you realize what could have happened to you?" Ambrosio said.

At least Pinocchio had the decency to say, "Yes." Then he added, "Don't think I'm ungrateful. I'm not. You did save my life and I'm..."

In the meantime a cheer rang through the square. The crowd was carrying the winning jockey.

"And you're...Finish the sentence..." said Ambrosio.

"I'm going to reward you. I know I could have been killed. Yes, you saved my life. So I'm going to give you, I promise, half of everything I have...."

By now Pinocchio was holding my hand. I saw the man looking down at our clasped hands.

"No no no," Ambrosio said. "That's not necessary. I don't need money, items, possessions, gifts...But I would just like to have half of..."

"Yes. What?"

The man with the expressionless face looked at me and said: "Her."

"Half of her? Half of Tinocchia. No, that's not fair."

"You promised. You said half of everything you have. You have her. I want half." And Ambrosio didn't even smile to indicate he was joking.

"Are you crazy? You saved me from being killed for this? Why didn't just let me die? I can't cut her in half. And, besides, Tinocchia is a puppetta."

"Don't you think I have eyes? Half of her is perfectly fine with me. Better half a puppetta than a whole girl."

And then I remembered that famous Bible scene where King Solomon judges between two women who claim one baby. The king calls for a sword. And for the baby. For the sake of fairness, he decides, the baby would be cut in two and each woman would get half the baby. One mother thought the ruling fair, but the other begged

Solomon, "Give the baby to her. Just don't kill him!" Hearing this, the wise King Solomon declares the second woman the true mother, for she was willing to give up her baby if that was necessary to save its life.

"Cutting her in half? You're out of your mind."

"That's up to you. All of her is fine with me too."

"Nothing doing, Ambrosio," Pinocchio said.

"I won't accept that. A human being must keep his word," said Ambrosio.

"Well, I'm not a human being."

"I don't care what you are. Probably a worm. But a promise is a promise. And don't forget I saved your life."

"I'm beginning to regret that." And then Pinocchio put his right index finger to his cheek. After thinking for a moment or two he called out, "Wait. I have an idea."

He turned to me and whispered into my ear.

"Sounds good, Pinocchio," I said. "We can explore it."

"What's your idea?" Ambrosio asked.

"I'll go you one better on the half of Tinocchia."

"How?"

"Have patience," Pinocchio said. Oh, the craftiness of his eyes. "Come back to Tinocchia's house with us."

"Do you promise, Pinocchio? I mean a real promise this time?"

"I promise. To keep my promise. I don't have a reputation as a liar, you know." . . .

"Hey, that's not fair," Pinocchio said. "What do you mean you want half of her? And besides, can't you see she's a puppetta?"

"I've got eyes, and a puppetta is fine with me," said Ambrosio, the man with the impassive face. "In civilized society a promise is a promise."

Pinocchio looked at me. I was wondering what he would say. He remained silent but looked hurt.

I cupped my hand over his left ear and whispered a few words. I also said, "It's an old Jewish custom to match people up."

Pinocchio brightened, laughed, and smiled.

"Tell him," I said. "Tell Ambrosio the good news."

Pinocchio stretched out his hands, as if addressing a crowd.

"I'll go you one better. Or, rather, half better. Fifty percent better. When we get back, instead of half a Tinocchia, you can have an entire Tinocchia."

"That's not fifty percent better," Ambrosio said happily. "That's one hundred percent better. Or doubly better."

"I was never good at arithmetic," Pinocchio said. "That's my offer."

Ambrosio looked at me. He looked at Pinocchio, then back at me, as if to say, What's your opinion of all this?

I nodded.

Ambrosio, the man with the odd blank face, made a little moue with his mouth, turning his lips down, puzzled and astonished.

... We were now in Papa Yossi's workshop. Here Pinocchio told Ambrosio:

"You asked for half of Tinocchia. But as I said I'm going to double it. I'm going to give you fifty percent more."

"But that's only seventy-five percent. It doesn't add up."

"My intentions are better than my arithmetic," Pinocchio said.

"I can see that," Ambrosio said, annoyed.

"What I'm trying to say is you asked for half of Tinocchia."

"Yes?"

"Well, you can have all of her."

While they were speaking, I withdrew. Ambrosio didn't see me leaving. I went into a little storeroom where Papa Yossi kept planks of sawed pine. Oh, the delicious aroma of freshly cut wood. I left the door slightly ajar so i could watch and listen.

Pinocchio took Ambrosio to a little side room where Tua stayed. He opened the door. She was reading a book.

"Hey, what's she doing here?" Ambrosio said. "She just was over there."

"She's quick... Anyway, here she is. She's all yours. The only problem is the exchange."

Tua stood and looked at Ambrosio. She stretched out her hand to greet him and shook his hand.

"What's the problem?" he said.

"In exchange for having all of her she lost the ability to talk. And you can call her by her nickname, Tua... Tua, this is Ambrosio... He's going to be your new friend...." Pinocchio turned back to the man. "Just remember, she can't talk."

"Who said so?" Tua said.

Well, this was a surprise. Tua speaking. I almost cried out, How wonderful, from my hiding place. I was so glad that Papa had agreed to my request to not disassemble her.

"So you can talk," Pinocchio said. "That's such good news."

"Well, I learned by listening," Tua said. Then she addressed Ambrosio. "May I see your face, Ambrosio?"

Curt Leviant

"How do you know what you're looking at is not my face?"

What Tua said next astonished us all.

"A puppetta can spot a fellow puppetto even through a mask."

"You're right," said Ambrosio. "But even your smart puppetti friends weren't able to do that."

And at once he peeled off the pseudo real face mask he had been wearing all along and revealed himself as a puppetto, and a good-looking one too, just like Pinocchio. No wonder I thought he had that impassive, expressionless face. It was his mask that did it.

"I was so happy to see a fellow puppetto at the Palio," Ambrosio continued, "and I couldn't bear the thought that one of them, you, Pinocchio, was quite ready to commit suicide."

"I appreciate it, Ambrosio. I really do.You saved my life...But why, when you saw we were also puppettos, why didn't you reveal yourself."

"I don't know. I guess I was ashamed. That's why I wear a face mask."

"Nothing to be ashamed of," said Pinocchio. "We're proud that we're puppettos."

"I can see that and I'm going to learn from you."

"Where are you from?" Pinocchio asked.

"I'm from Milano. I came down to Siena specially to see the Palio. And I never dreamt that I would encounter another talking puppetto."

"And who made you?"

"A woodworker by the name of Primo."

Now Ambrosio stretched his hand out to Tua and said, "Would you like to come with me?"

Tua looked at him. By now I had come out of the other room. She looked at me and asked, "Is it all right?"

"Of course,Tua," I said. "I'm so happy you can talk. And even happier that you found a friend."

"Wait a minute," Ambrosio said, looking at Tua and me.

"There's two of you."

"When you leave with Tua, there will be one of us," I said.

"Well, Tua is certainly a good choice. I've been looking for a lovely puppetta for years," Ambrosio said. "No harm meant, but between the two of you she has that spark in her eyes."

Hearing this, Tua beamed.

"And I'm so happy you found a wonderful partner who appreciates you. Now you won't be lonely any more, Tua, for you'll have someone with you all the time."

"But I should ask Yossi too," she said.

"He's not home now. But don't worry. I'll tell him. And some day when we are in Milan we will look for Primo's workshop and come to see you."

Tua came up to me, embraced me, and kissed my cheek. "Thank you for being so nice to me. And tell Yossi I thank him too."

She gave her hand to Ambrosio, who said, "Well, this is an unbelievable turn of events. I came to see a horse race and found a puppetta. And one hundred percent of one at that."

At the door they turned to wave goodbye and then they walked out of the house together.

46
The Mayor's Report on the Priest's Signs

About a week after Tua and Ambrosio had gone, the Mayor came to our house with a surprising report.

This is what he said:

"Giuseppe, I just met the priest on the street. You know we always greet each other cordially, even though we're on opposite sides of the fence, so to speak. He's a complex chap, a devoted servant of the church, sometimes rigid, but, as you saw after the debate, there is a streak of niceness in him, which, occasionally, it even seems he can't help it, overrides his fanaticism. Anyway, I asked him to explain to me the signs he had given you during the silent debate and how he interpreted your signs in reply. But before I tell you what he said why don't you share with me, Giuseppe, how *you* interpreted his signs and what you meant by yours."

My father responded:

"Of course, Giorgio." And Papa stood, just as he had during the debate, even assuming the same stance. "You remember, for the first sign the priest lit a match. This had me puzzled, but I looked at Tinocchia and she very subtly brought her fist to her mouth and tilted back her head, giving me a wordless sign about drinking water. Then I understood what Antonio was saying and what I should say in reply. It seemed he was telling me, I can burn down your workshop. To answer him without words, and thanks to clever Tinocchia, I poured out my flask of water on the ground toward him to show him I am prepared to fight fire with water, for with wood all around me in the workshop I always fear fire and that's why I have lots of pails of water ready. Then, for the second sign, the priest looked at me through a piece of glass to indicate he can watch me. So I pulled out the magic pinhole mirror that I made. By so doing, I showed him that with this mirror I can see him *and* myself, whereas he can only see me. I could tell by the expression on his face that my good answer upset him. Because for the third sign Antonio pointed one finger at me as if to say he would poke out one of my eyes. So in reply I pointed *two* fingers at him to show if he did that I'd take out both of his eyes."

The Mayor clapped his hands once in astonishment and laughed heartily.

"Mama mia! What a difference between your interpretations of the signs and the priest's. Listen to what he told me. Antonio said he lit a match to show you that all non-believers, by which he meant you, and probably a lapsed Catholic atheist like me, that is, all non-believers, will suffer the fires of hell. In response, you took out your water flask and poured it on the ground. The priest took that to mean that you wanted to show that the second Great Flood, like in Noah's time, will put out those fires.

"Then, for the second sign, Antonio took out his piece of glass and looked through it. He told me he meant to show that we have to see, to notice, others. Then you took out your mirror and flashed it. According to the priest, by this you declared that if a person looks only into a mirrored glass, he will see only himself and never others. Then you looked into the mirror and the priest took that to mean that before we see others we have to look into ourselves.

"Finally, for the third sign, Antonio raised one finger and shook it, pointing to the sky. He told me he wanted to say we have one king. You answered by raising two fingers. He thought your reply was that there are two kings, one in heaven and one on earth... So, no matter what the interpretations, you beat him, bravo, Giuseppe, and he himself admitted it... I'm so glad you won, dear Giuseppe. That rascal should never have summoned you in the first place."

To which Yossi replied: "But like Rabbino dei Rossi told

me when I reported this to him right after the debate, the priest admitted defeat because we're in modern Italy, not in Torquemada's Spain. We Italians are a different people."

"You're right, Giuseppe, and we're all proud of that."

"And thank you, my dear friend, Giorgio, for this surprising report."

But Giorgio's surprise could in no way match the astonishment that overwhelmed me the next time I saw Pinocchio.

47
Pinocchio's Visit

One day Pinocchio came to visit me. None of my adventures nor any of Pinocchio's previous adventures could match the events of that day. I looked at the puppetto. Something was off kilter. It was and it wasn't Pinocchio. I recognized his nose – but I hardly recognized the rest of him. His face had changed. There was color in his cheeks. No longer were his lips thin. Those thin wooden lips that had kissed me long ago.

"Don't you recognize me?" he said.

"Well, sort of..."

"Can't you see what's happened? Don't just stare at my nose. Look at the rest of me."

"You're different."

"Yes, but how?" Pinocchio took one step closer to me. "Will you look at *me*, for goodness' sake? And not just at my nose? What do you see?"

"I see..." I said hesitantly, "color in your cheeks..."

"What else?"

I wasn't quite sure. There was Pinocchio, different. But still with his familiar nose.

"It's taking you too long," he said impatiently. "I might as well tell you. Otherwise, we'll be talking in circles. Look at this, Tinocchia."

Pinocchio stretched out his fingers and pointed to the veins on the back of his hands.

"Can't you see the difference?" he continued. Now he stood on tiptoes, raised his hands, and spread them out. And he said proudly, he almost shouted, "I'm a real boy now."

"I knew I sensed something different but I couldn't tell what. That delicious fragrance of pinewood, that was gone... But your nose..."

"I purposely kept my old nose. Asked Geppetto for that. As a reminder of who I was...really am....And you? What about you, Tinocchia, have you thought of becoming a real girl?"

I didn't want to tell him that I wanted to live, and that's why I wanted to remain a puppetta.

"If I do, will I too have to be swallowed by a huge fish, like you?"

"You're joking," Pinocchio said.

Sometimes the best answer is no answer. I just looked at the puppetto without saying a word, neither feigning innocence nor giving any indication of tongue in cheek.

Then Pinocchio continued:

"A fish has nothing to do with it. You just have to go to school, love homework, be respectful of others and, in general, be a nice person."

But now I couldn't tell if he was being serious or not, parodying Collodi's vision of a good puppetto. I thought about it for a minute and decided: he was parodying, the rascal. He couldn't be serious for two minutes in a row. And, what's more, he made absolutely no mention of telling the truth as one of the criteria for becoming a real boy.

"But I already do all of that," I said. But then, because I thought I was bragging, I added in a self-mocking tone, "Can't you see I'm perfect?"

"Then maybe you're not naughty enough. You have to have some bad qualities to improve from. Take lessons from me. I will be your private Tutor of Naughtiness."

"How much do you charge?"

"Either five gold coins or one kiss," Pinocchio said.

"Shall I lie and say No?"

And we both laughed. Pinocchio took hold of my fingers, touching them, as if looking to see if the coins were already there, or if by some chance my fingers were already those of a real girl.

I looked the former puppetto up and down. "Tell me, how did

you do it?"

"It's not me. Geppetto did it."

Then another thought flew through my mind. A nasty one, one prompted by jealousy. There was another reason for him becoming a real boy and I knew just what it was. And I didn't hold back from saying:

"You did this to pursue your romance with Zeresh."

"Are you at that again? Will you stop that? With that anti-Semite?"

"I thought you once said some of your best friends are Persian anti-Semites."

"I'll disregard that remark as one of your jokes. But please leave Zeresh out of this. Me becoming a real boy was Geppetto's idea. His reward to me."

Pinocchio looked sincere, but I was still skeptical. I had long stopped looking at his nose. I felt it wasn't fair. I could check him but he couldn't check me.

"But I can go back anytime I want."

"To her?"

"No." Pinocchio laughed. "I can go back to being a puppetto."

Now I couldn't resist. I watched his nose.

He wasn't lying.

"You can? Really? Really and truly? Honestly, you can?"

"Yes."

I made a face to show I was skeptical.

"But how? You still didn't tell me how you made the transformation."

"It's a secret."

At once I spun around, angry, and turned my back to him.

"Again showing me your back. Boy, you get upset so quickly."

"Very nice." I turned around. "Keeping a secret from your best friend."

"All right, I'll tell you, but I'm not supposed to... It's a secret. A secret salve."

Curt Leviant

My reaction was quick. "I can't believe such a silly ointment exists. If so, then every wooden dummy can become a real person."

"True, but it doesn't make them any less a dummy."

How right he was I soon found out.

"I don't believe it. A secret salve."

"You don't have to believe it. All you got to do is look at me."

And once again he showed me and moved all his nimble fingers. With his index finger he flicked the lobe of his left ear, and then flicked the ear itself, which made a dull resonant sound like a far-off drum.

"So tell me, Tinocchia, am I a puppetto or a real boy?"

I looked at him again. Brown hair, real hair, with a forelock dangling over his forehead. Brown, dancing, very mobile eyes. I put my fingers to his face and slowly tugged at his cheek.

"Yes, you're quite real. But how did you deserve this?"

"Geppetto promised me that if I did well in school, kept tricks to a minimum, and behaved like a good boy, he would apply the secret salve. And he kept his promise...Come, I'll show you the salve. It's in Geppetto's workshop."

Pinocchio took me by the hand.

I could hardly keep pace with him he walked so quickly now. He kept running ahead and turning and urging me to walk faster.

"I can't. I'm doing the best I can. I don't have your kind of legs, you know."

"Maybe when you see the secret salve you'll want some too."

That scared me, that remark, that scared me. A strange, an odd feeling ran through me. A sudden malaise in my head and stomach, a weakness in my legs.

In the house Pinocchio opened the door to his father's workshop. You know I love the smell of wood, the fragrance of it, the various aromas each kind of wood gives off, the cut boards, the shavings, even the sawdust, mostly of pine – my kin. It was like for other people a trail in the woods, walking under pine trees, the refreshing smell of grass, moss and leaves. Here in the workshop the wood, especially the pine, was like a breath of fresh air for me.

Suddenly, before me Pinocchio held a little glass dish filled with a soft, honey-colored substance akin to molten wax. I still saw the imprint of a couple of fingers in it.

"This is the magic salve. Would you like to try it?"

Pinocchio was about to dip his fingers into the dish.

"Stop!" I yelled.

An elemental fear – terror – as if I were about to die, gripped my throat. A feeling I'd never had before shook me to my inmost being. I felt that what I was, my essence, my me-ness, was being sucked out of me. It came in pulses in my body. My knees about to buckle. I sensed a sadness in me, bigger than me. Huge butterfly wings flitted weakly in my heart. A heavy shadow in me squeezing, choking the me-ness out of me. As if in a dream, no, a nightmare, I was being pulled, tugged, drawn out of this world. I felt the Tree of Life being cut from under me, limb by limb. I was dying. I didn't think one could feel that sensation. I always thought death came suddenly. And now, with me, it was coming slowly, possessing me, and I wanted to stop it. I wanted to live, to live. If I didn't take hold of myself, I sensed Tinocchia would disappear.

"What's wrong with you?" I screamed. At least I thought I screamed. But it came out as a loud, hoarse whisper. "That's not your salve. It's Geppetto's. You can't, you shouldn't touch it or ever go near it without his permission." Now my voice came back and I shouted, "Don't you dare touch it! I'm ashamed of you, Pinocchio. I thought your papa made you a real boy because you've been good. But I see you don't deserve what he did for you. Do you want him to regret he made you a boy?"

Pinocchio paled at my words. He opened his mouth but he couldn't speak. This was the first time I had ever seen him so beaten down.

A door slammed.

"Papa. He's home," Pinocchio said in a low, weak voice.

At once Pinocchio put the dish away.

But he couldn't resist saying, "You missed your chance."

"And you missed yours." Again I was barely able to sound out the words. "Geppetto should never have made you real. Because you haven't learned a thing. You're still a wooden blockhead. You're just the same. Nothing has changed."

"You could have become a girl."

"Talking to you is like talking to the wall. Or to a chunk of wood. You're not getting the point, Pinocchio. Even if I wanted to I would have to get permission from Yossi and from Geppetto."

Just then Geppetto came in to the workshop.

"Ah, Tinocchia, how nice to see you...Well, what do you think of our new boy?"

I didn't know what to say. I was still upset at what Pinocchio had done. And that feeling of life ebbing out of me still there. And I kept saying to myself, You don't deserve it, Pinocchio. You don't deserve it. That magic salve that could make wood flesh and blood – it was still sending strange shivers running through me. And that elemental fright still gripped me. And then it came back to me with a gloomy rush of wind: That Dark Angel with the word *sam*, Hebrew for 'poison', built into his name.

I just nodded to Geppetto and gave him a twilight half smile.

"The only thing I left from his puppetto state was his nose. This way I can still check on his truth-telling."

At this I looked at Pinocchio. That's not what he told me about half an hour ago, when the puppetto said it was his decision to keep his nose to remind him of his former state, apparently as a check on his pride.

Geppetto put his pinkie and forefinger on Pinocchio's nose and asked:

"Been doing any fibbing lately?"

"No," Pinocchio said.

Geppetto laughed, holding the tip of his son's wooden nose. "The wood is pressing into my index finger, you rascal!"

Then Geppetto put his hands on his hips and said to me,

"Well, what do you say, big little girl? Would you like to change too?"

Geppetto's words made me feel even more queasy. That elemental fear of life being sucked out of me had not yet gone away. With Geppetto's question that fright, that melancholia, intensified. Was this just a polite remark, like little children are asked, What would you like to do when you grow up? Or was Geppetto offering me a life-changing opportunity? I was as afraid as if I'd wandered in the dark into an ogre's lair. I felt I was choking. A shadow, like an umber curtain, slid over me. My eyes darkened. Yes, the fear of death. I put my hands to my eyes and said over and over, "I can't...I can't...I can't..."

And what if that magic salve would just take me away and not do anything else, just remove the me-ness of me?

"I can't," I cried, scared to death, shaking and crying.

"Hush, hush, darling girl," Geppetto said. He put his hands around me, drew me close, and kissed me tenderly on the forehead. "Don't cry, don't be afraid...I understand...I understand...I'm sorry. I shouldn't have...It really wasn't... It's too..."

And he fell silent without finishing the sentence.

Pinocchio walked me home. Wisely, he did not say a word.

I wanted to think that Pinocchio had regretted what he had done. But I couldn't be sure. I was trembling too much to think clearly. But I had enough presence of mind to realize that within fifteen to twenty minutes two people had offered to transform me. Maybe Geppetto's remark was just a general one, which his three words, "It really wasn't" verified. Very likely he meant to say, "It really wasn't an offer to do for you what I did for Pinocchio." Maybe he was apologizing for even saying it was a thoughtless remark.

Still, I could not be sure. And that's why I'm still trembling.

But one thing I learned.

A leopard can't change his spots.

Changing Pinocchio from a puppetto to a boy, giving him

bendable ears, did not change his personality.

And maybe I learned something else. Perhaps Pinocchio liked the idea of being a real boy so that he could cuddle up to Zeresh. Even though he had called her an anti-Semite, if she liked him as a wooden boy what would she think of him as a real one? I can't even refer to her by her real Italian name, Neschina. In my mind she will always be the evil Zeresh, mate of the hateful Haman.

And then I remembered: it was Pinocchio who played Haman in the Purim-shpil.

48
Geppetto Tells Tinocchia How He Got the Salve

That magic salve that Pinocchio showed me and which upset me so much, I couldn't get it out of my mind. I wanted to ask Geppetto how he got it. But then I thought, this might be private, so I held back. But then I reconsidered. If I don't ask now I will always regret not knowing. An awful feeling: I could have asked but didn't. So I spoke up.

Geppetto answered right away.

"A man who called himself a messenger gave it to me," Geppetto said. "And since this was such an unusual experience, I decided to write it down because I didn't want to forget it. I wanted to remember it word for word." He went to a cabinet, took out a piece of paper, and handed it to me. I was impressed with Geppetto's careful, precise script, which reflected the care he took with his work.

"Here. Tinocchia. Read it."

A knock on my door and then this man who looked like any of us, nothing special, nothing unusual about him, came in. He told me he had heard about Pinocchio, the wooden puppetto whom I had made. And he said he had something for me, a salve that I could apply to make him a real boy.

"Are you an angel?" I asked.

"No," he said.

"A wizard?"

Again he said, "No...I just told you. I'm a messenger."

"And you're not a magician?"

Then the man became impatient with me and did not answer. Still, I asked him, "What's your name?"

He said, "I can't give it to you... It's a wonder."

At this point I spoke up and told Geppetto:

"In the Bible, the man who comes to the parents of Samson to announce Samson's birth says the same thing. He says he's a messenger but everyone knows he's an angel."

Geppetto smiled and nodded. "Keep reading... I told him the same story."

"You probably know about the messenger who came to Samson's parents."

"Well," the man said, "If you're asking in a roundabout way if I am that sort of man, I will answer in a roundabout way and say I am not answering."

"For a messenger," I said, "you're rather quiet."

He looked at me for a moment then said softly:

"Messengers act, deliver, do. They are not talkers. They're sparing with words. And my job now is to give you a salve you can use on your puppetto, Pinocchio, whenever you feel he is ready to become a full- fledged boy... Just rub it gently on him, from top to toe."

I thanked Geppetto for sharing this with me, but even just reading these words about the magic salve prompted that odd feeling that I had had when Pinocchio showed it to me and asked if I want to use it: my life being slowly drawn out of me, like Yossi slowly pulling out a nail deeply embedded in wood.

But all this was just prelude to Pinocchio's surprising words when he saw me the next day.

49
Tinocchia Looks at Pinocchio

"Tinocchia," Pinocchio said. "I want to tell you something...I'm afraid...Afraid of dying."

"What? What's this all of a sudden?" I said. "Remember when in your book you were talking to the fairy? When she tried to give you bitter medicine, you said you were not afraid of death."

"That was then and this is now. Then I was in a book. Now I'm in the real world. Now I am afraid, for I see what it means to be human," Pinocchio said with a gloomy tone in his voice.

But then a tender glow lit his eyes as he murmured, "But there's also another thing. Even more important. I want to stay with you. And be like you. Like I once was."

A wave of warmth went through me. I felt a tug in my eyes.

"But you're already a boy now... I don't understand... Don't you want to be a normal real boy any more?"

"No."

Now I watched his nose with care. It did not budge.

"And what about you, Tinocchia, don't you want to become a regular flesh-and-blood girl?"

"No. Not at all." I looked him straight in the eye. "Don't you remember how even the thought of it upset me, scared me near to death? When you brought me to Geppetto's workshop and showed me the magic salve? And even when Geppetto asked me if I want to... No. I don't want to. No, no, and no again. Your views are my views exactly."

We looked at each other; both of us were silent.

"So what are you going to do?" I asked Pinocchio.

"Go back," he said at once. "Return."

"Really?"

"Yes. Really."

"For me?"

"For you."

"Can you?"

"I'm sure I can. In fact, I know I can."

"How do you know?"

"Remember, I have a couple of wishes left from the three I was given."

Then the seriousness of this struck me. It actually hit me like a blow in the heart.

In my thoughts I heard again: I want to stay with you.

"Are you sure you can switch back?"

"Yes, if the wishes still work... And if not, I can always use the magic salve in Geppetto's workshop."

Irritated, again I burst out with, "But we went over that. We spoke about how not nice, unethical, it is to use that salve without permission. I told you that already. It isn't right. It's not yours. You were made a real boy because Geppetto considered you good, worthy. And now you're going back to being a rascally puppetto again. It's just not ni – "

"There you go again talking too much. Preaching again. You sound just like Collodi. Why don't you just keep quiet. I wish you'd shut up."

At once I felt a rush of soundless wind – a wave like a towel being snapped in the air. I opened my mouth, but no sounds came. My tongue was paralyzed.

"Oh, my God!" Pinocchio cried out, clasping his mouth with his palm. "I just wasted one of my wishes." He fell on his knees, both hands on his heart. "I'm sorry. I'm so sorry."

I took a piece of paper, found a pencil, and wrote:

"Now you have one wish left."

"All right, then, for my last wish... I wish..."

Quicker than quick my right hand shot forth to Pinocchio's mouth. I did what he had done a moment earlier with the palm of his own hand. I stopped him from wasting his last wish. With my index finger up, signaling wait, I wrote:

"Don't! I have a great idea for you. For your third wish ask for three more wishes."

"What?!... But... But..."

And I continued to write:

"No buts. There are no rules. It's just a convention in fairy tales. We don't have to be slaves to the fairy tales, and we don't have to be bound by the ridiculous world of make-believe."

I was about to tell him that was precisely what I had done, but I held back. He would ask me what my extra wishes were and I didn't want to share that with him.

I wrote: "Just ask for three more wishes and use the first to free my tongue."

"Okay, that's a good idea." But the words were mechanically said. I could see he wasn't convinced. Nevertheless, Pinocchio closed his eyes and said ardently:

"For my third wish I wish for three more wishes."

He opened his eyes and waited. I don't know what was happening with Pinocchio but I felt little bubbles running over my skin.

"And for my first wish, restore Tinocchia's ability to speak."

Again, I felt a surge in me, an inner rush of energy, which rose to my mouth and lips. First, I whispered, "Thanks" and heard that softly uttered word. Then out loud, "Thank you, Pinocchio. It worked."

"Wow! How did you think of that great idea? I always knew about three wishes but I never dreamt that the third wish could be used that way."

"You see, every time I read in a fairy tale that the good fairy gave someone three wishes and he used all three up I would say, you dummy, for the third wish why don't you ask for three more wishes. But no one ever did."

"Except you," Pinocchio said.

Thinking of the extra wishes, I asked Pinocchio.

"Did you ever wish for the good health of your father?"

This stung. He looked abashed.

"You're right. I should have. And I will."

For a moment we were silent. Again I was assessing the situation.

"So you really want to switch back?"

"Yes."

"And really for me?"

"For you."

Then it struck me. "But Pinocchio, you're not Jewish."

I thought of adding "even" after the "not" but decided that would make him feel bad. And you played Haman in the Purim-shpil. But that would make him feel worse. And in your role you even put a human face on Haman when you improvised and laid the blame on your wife, Zeresh. But that would make him feel absolutely rotten. And it was I who encouraged him to try out for the Purim-shpil.

Pinocchio touched his long wooden nose, the only thing that remained from his former puppetto state.

"I'll circumscribe it."

From his pocket he took a penknife and began to whittle the edge of his nose. The long slivers of white pine, fine and thin, flew off like tiny light beige butterflies, one chasing the other. It didn't seem to hurt Pinocchio, but it pained me as if skin from my nose were being sliced.

"Stop!" I shouted and held on to his nice Jewish nose. It seemed warm to the touch, bruised, and slightly red. I guess there was something human, real, about it after all.

"I like it the way it is," I said, looking at his nose with admiration. Then I added: "It's something else you'll have to circumcise."

To this Pinocchio made no response – but he did put the penknife away and I was glad of that. I brushed from his nose the few tiny remaining flecks of sawdust the size of grains of salt.

"I'll convert," he said.

"How many conversions can you undertake? Puppetto to real boy, boy to puppetto, non-Jew to Jew."

"Because next year I want to play Mordecai, not Haman," the

rascal said, his eyes twinkling, sparkling, real live mischief glistening in every pore of his face.

"I don't know if you realize it, Pinocchio, but you have two lives. A double life. You have an eternal life in your book, a world masterpiece that will live forever, with you as hero in it. And you have your life here, in the real world."

"I never thought of it that way. You sure have a wonderful way of looking at things, Tinocchia, as if you have a glass with lots of mirrors inside of you."

And then the puppetto added:

"Even if you don't think I'm Jewish, there's a but...Listen to this. In fact, I may even be Jewish. Geppetto once told me that his grandmother was a red-haired beauty with green eyes. It turns out she was adopted. Nobody ever said a word about where she came from, her origins, and so forth. My father tells me she had some special sayings which may have been Yiddish, and one day every year, around the end of September, she didn't eat or drink but fasted the entire day."

"But that doesn't make you Jewish."

"True, but I'm getting close. In any case, I will convert."

"Why?"

"Because I want to be on your side. On Esther's. Not on Haman's."

I could have hugged him for that answer.

And I did.

With a proud, puckish smile on his face, Pinocchio said:

"Tinocchia, before I return I want to ask you once again, Are you sure you don't want to be a girl?"

"Yes. I am sure."

"Not even for a little bit?"

"No. Not at all."

"But why?"

"I told you. I share your views. I don't want mortality. I want to live. Being a puppetta is like remaining between the pages of a book forever. This way you always live. The other way you get sick and suffer and die."

"But..." Pinocchio interrupted.

"There are no buts. I've seen the real people around me. If I pinch you, like this, it hurts..."

"Ow!"

"... doesn't it? But if you pinch me, I don't feel a thing."

"But there are other things you can feel as a human being and can do, like..."

I saw he was hesitating, afraid to say it, but I knew what he wanted to say.

"Go, Pinocchio. Go ahead and say it."

"Like giving birth."

"I know," I said sadly, "but still I would like to continue to eat from the Tree of Life."

50
Tinocchia's Test

The next time I saw Pinocchio I had something prepared for him.

"All right, Pinocchio. You say you like me. I want to test that affection."

Instead of saying, Yes, even if reluctantly, that wooden scoundrel said:

"You mean a test like in the storybook romances where the lover has to climb a mountain, battle dragons, kill ogres, and otherwise commit suicide to prove his love?" Pinocchio shook his head. "Count me out."

I laughed. "No. It's not that romantic. Or that dangerous. Or even that hard."

"Fine. Tell me what I have to do."

Since I couldn't remember all of the tasks, I took out a piece of paper and read from it.

"Here they are. I want you to show me the horn of a wolf, the milk of a chicken, the juice of a marble slab, the shadow of a pit, and one ounce of moonlight."

"Hey, wait! That's five. In folktales the hero is only given three tests."

"Then show me three of them," I said.

Pinocchio took the list from my hand, looked at it, and grimaced.

"Even one is impossible and you know it. This is right out of a children's storybook. You said it wouldn't be hard. Shadow of a pit. Ounce of moonlight. Crazy! This is even harder than killing an ogre."

"Pinocchio," I said. "You have a good imagination. I leave it to you to see how close you can come to fulfilling this task and show me at least three."

"Make me a copy of the list."

I did and gave it to him.

51
Tinocchia Asks Pinocchio a Question

When Pinocchio visited two days later, I thought he would surely say something about the tasks I had imposed on him. I looked at him and waited. I don't recall if I assumed an impatient stance, hands crossed on my chest, and a grumpy look on my face. In any case, he said nothing, evidently waiting for me to speak. But I didn't want to bring up the subject. Had he found a solution to the tasks he would have told me at once. Instead, I decided to ask him:

"Pinocchio, do you think I'm pretty?"

"Do you think I'm much good at thinking? Didn't you once call me a wooden blockhead?"

"Then don't think. Say! Answer! Am I pretty?"

"Which of these two questions am I supposed to answer? Am I pretty? Or, Do you think I'm pretty?"

"You're impossible, Pinocchio. What do you see when you look at me?"

But the rascal came back with:

"What do *you* see when you look in the mirror?"

Insulted, peeved, I wheeled about and turned my back to him. But since I couldn't remain silent much longer, I said over my shoulder:

"Can't you answer a question, you foolish wooden blockhead puppetto, without asking another question?"

"Who says I can't? And how come you always turn your back when you're mad?"

Now I faced him.

"When I ask you if I'm pretty, why do you twist my question around and ask me what I see when I look in the mirror?"

"Why not?"

"It seems you are totally incapable of answering a question

without asking one in turn."

"What makes you say that?"

I stamped my foot and ran out. I knew Pinocchio was teasing me but I still didn't like it.

At the doorway I shouted to him:

"You know what I recommend to you?"

"What?"

"You better ask Geppetto to make you over again, this time with a better recipe."

"You think he'll agree?"

"I can't wait to see you as Haman," I shouted. "That fits you perfectly."

And as I slammed the door I heard him say:

"But won't you still have to invite me to your royal dinner, Queen Esther?"

52
Pinocchio's Return

Just like in folktales Pinocchio came back on the third day. There was a smile on his face. That looked like a good sign. Still, with Pinocchio it was hard to tell. He was such a good actor. In any case, he held nothing. In fact, his hands were deep in his pockets. So how could he have fulfilled his test?

"Well?"

"Well, first of all I want to apologize for teasing you the other day."

"This is something new. You? Apologizing? I guess the quest has done something to you. I almost regretted sending you out to prove to me you liked me."

Pinocchio looked down at the wooden floor.

"Okay. Enough of that. You were smiling when you came in. Is that a good sign?"

"I think I've succeeded."

"I told you I have confidence in your imagination. So what have you got for me? And where are they?"

From his shirt pocket Pinocchio took a piece of paper almost the same size as the one I had given him.

"Here, Tinocchia. Luckily, you didn't say, Bring me. You said, Show me. So here it is... I'm showing you."

"But this is in Hebrew. You don't know Hebrew."

"But you do. And so does Rabbino dei Rossi."

"What does the rabbino have to do with this?"

"Very simple," Pinocchio said. "All these impossible combinations, like wolf's horn or chicken's milk, sounded like something out of a folktale. I figured the rabbino, who is an educated man, would know this. So I went to him and told him why I had come. Soon as I showed him the list he smiled and said, 'You're in luck. I know exactly where all this comes from. It's from a rhymed prose Hebrew story by a thirteenth century Roman poet. His name is Immanuel of Rome. It just so happens I've been re-reading his wonderful work. What's more, in our family we have a tradition passed down from father to son that we are descendants of this famous writer. And so I'm very familiar with and proud of his writings.' That's what the rabbino said."

"So these Hebrew lines are in the rabbino's handwriting."

"Yes. He copied down the lines with those five absurd combinations right out of Immanuel of Rome's story. And I actually saw the book."

"Amazing," I said.

"Now let me ask you, Tinocchia, how you got to these crazy things. The rabbino also wanted to know how you know this but I couldn't answer."

"I must have read these somewhere in a folktale. And I had no idea they come from Hebrew literature and from right here in Italy. They've probably been floating around European folklore for centuries."

Then I went over and hugged Pinocchio. "You passed the test."

"Come on," he said, "did you really think I could accomplish this impossible task?"

"I told you I had faith in your imagination. And I was right."

"Fine. But what if I didn't pass?"

I laughed. "Do you think I would like you any less, you pinewood rascal? It was just a game. Right out of a folktale — but without the dangerous or dire, dire consequences."

Then I took him by the hand.

53
And if We Get...

"And if we get married," Pinocchio said quickly, hoping I would not contradict him, "and we want children, I would ask Giuseppe and Geppetto to get together and create a little puppetto for us, and we would help them. We would make a boy puppetto and name him Tinocchio..."

"... and while we do this, perhaps a year or two later, we will all make a lovely girl puppetta and name her..."

"... Pinocchia!" Pinocchio said enthusiastically, blushing, even to the length of his wooden nose. He removed his hand from mine and raised both his arms.

By now it was dusk, the beneficent dusk of a clear cloudless twilight. I looked at the darkening horizon. A faint light was glowing there, slowly, gradually brightening. I could have sworn I saw a few sparks of Yossi's daylight there. The daylight Yossi was going to beat out of that beautiful water imp, who had turned me into a swan – the daylight that is in all of us. Now a tiny arc of golden light, almost mist-like, shaped like a rainbow, was starting to peep out of the bottom of the sky.

Pinocchio slipped his hand into mine and, like two happy puppetti, hearing no music in the background except the music in our heads, we walked slowly to the so slow slowly ascending full – with its luminescent orange red glow, now big and round, a golden globe, suspended there as if it would remain just above the horizon forever and ever and never ever go away, enormous, so huge and beautiful, bigger than any sunset I've ever seen, filled with the *yehee or* of God's first command, folktale perfect, sun-mirrored, full – moon.

54

And they lived happily ever after.

Presumably,

for in fiction that borders reality nothing is predictable.

Or, as Tinocchia said in the Epigraph:

Everything is possible in an impossible world.

AFTERWORD
IN THE VENICE OLD AGE HOME

A week or so after I finished my research at the Siena Munic-ipal Library and had copied the story of Tinocchia, still not sure who had written it, I went to Venice, my favorite Italian city, to relax for a few days.

One evening, while visiting the Ghetto, I went to the Jew-ish community's Old Age Home and had dinner in the dining room, which is open to the public. Only seven residents lived in this rather large old building. I was the sole guest. The elderly five women and two men looked at me with curiosity until the manager, with whom I had spoken earlier, introduced me. He said I was an American schol-ar who specialized in Italian Jewish culture, loved Italian folklore, and was fluent in Italian.

"Soon," he added, "our guest will begin to translate into En-glish a long Italian story he has just discovered in a library."

"A story. A story," one of the old women cried out. This call was taken up, with smiles, by all the people in the room.

"A story. A story. Tell us a story."

I thought that next, in unison, they would begin to bang their fists on the table and chant, "Story, story, story."

I blinked self-consciously and did not respond. Telling stories wasn't my usual line of work.

Now they fell silent, waiting.

Then, another woman, very likely the oldest in the room, tall and thin, with a distinguished face, repeated:

"Yes, can you tell us a story? My name is Violetta and I love stories."

Again came the happy chorus, "Story, story."

The manager tried to calm them. "Please. Please! Let our guest eat. Please don't disturb him."

But I nodded and indicated with my hands that it was all right.

I figured I'd tell them the story that I now knew by heart.

I rose and said in Italian:

"I will tell you the beginning of a nice Jewish children's story I have just finished reading. We don't know who wrote it. So we'll have to say it's anonymous. Here's how the story begins: Once upon a time..."

"No, no," the oldsters shouted, almost in the unison I had been expecting before, "not the beginning..."

"We're old," I heard one woman's voice.

"The end," Violetta said. "We want the end...I'm ninety-nine. We don't have time for beginnings. Beginnings do not interest us. Only endings."

I looked at Violetta. Ninety-nine? She didn't look it, had no signs of old age. I thought she was at most seventy-five. Her voice, no quavers; her brown eyes knowing; her demeanor sharp. An energy, a liveliness, bubbled out of her.

"The end, the end," the women repeated. The two men, I noticed, were silent. Perhaps out of vanity they didn't want to admit they were old.

I still remember the women's musical Italian.

"*Siamo vecchi*," one woman sang out – we're old – a proud little expression on her face as though she had uttered an original bon mot. Followed by Violetta's, "*Non abbiamo tempo per la genesi*." We don't have time for genesis, or beginnings, hinting at the Bible's opening words, "In the beginning God created the heavens and the earth."

"The end is what we want."

The manager and I exchanged glances. He shrugged, as if to say, What can I do?

"Okay," I said. "Here's the end of the story I just finished reading at the Siena Municipal Library. It's about a Jewish girl marionette or puppetta."

Soon as I said that the ninety-nine-year-old Violetta clapped her hands in glee, her big brown eyes wide open in astonishment.

I interrupted my narration. "What is it?"

"Oh my," she called. "Go on. I will tell you when you finish."

"No. Please tell me now. This must be something exciting."
But Violetta held her own.

"No no," she said. "Continue."

"Here's the ending of this Jewish story that takes place right here in Italy, in which there is also a humorous, rhymed Purim-shpil, or Purim play. The girl puppetta...." I figured the old folk wouldn't recognize or remember Tinocchia's name, and I didn't want to start explaining it, so I only mentioned the very recognizable Pinocchio, "befriended the famous Pinocchio who also appears in this story. By the end..." and I repeated the word, "by the end he is already a real boy, although he still tells lies once in a while and his nose gets longer. Pinocchio likes the girl puppetta and she likes him. She considers him charming, and there is a hint that he will convert and become Jewish, and he may even switch back and become a puppetto once again, and their love story ends like a good fairy tale and they live happily after.... The end!"

"Good, good," all seven of my listeners shouted and applauded. Violetta still looked excited, impatient to speak. I actually saw a roseate bloom on her cheeks. Full of curiosity, I waited to hear what she would say.

And what she said astonished me.

"Why didn't you say the puppetta's name was Tinocchia?"

In a non-existent mirror, maybe Papa Yossi's, I saw my jaw dropping in surprise.

"Wait a minute! How...?"

"Tell, tell..."

"Because it's too complicated a name..." I said, "and how... how do you know this?"

Violetta didn't answer right away. She held back, looked at the other residents, perhaps to enhance the drama.

Then she said:

"I come from Siena."

"This… this is so…" I stammered. "So you know the story?"

Violetta nodded once, a long slow assured nod.

"From?"

"My family name is Livorno."

"Oh, my Lord! This is…" and I shook my head in bewilderment. "Are you by any chance related to Abramo?"

Again she looked about. A moment later – one very long moment – she said:

"Yes."

Then silence. Not another word. Keeping the suspense alive.

"How?" I asked, looking intently at her, seeing only Violetta in the entire room.

Violetta smiled, a pleased, a happy smile. "My father."

Now I rose from my seat and approached her table.

"Was he also," said as I drew closer, sailing, no floor beneath me, "the beadle of the Siena synagogue?"

"No, no. Not the beadle." She looked up at me. "No, no. The cantor. The mention of the beadle is a purposeful distraction." Violetta looked at me with surprise. "Why are you standing? Why don't you sit down?"

"No wonder," I said as I sat down, "I couldn't find his name in that famous archives list of rabbis and beadles of the Siena Jewish Community."

"I know," Violetta said. "They stupidly recorded only the rabbis and beadles and not the cantors. Probably because cantors come and go. But my beloved father served as cantor for forty-six years."

"Abramo, right?"

"Yes. Abramo."

"The manuscript I found in the archives is not clear as to who the author is. That's why I said it's an anonymous work… Is it really your father's?"

Would she lie in response? Would her nose get longer?

Again Violetta did not answer right away. She seemed to be

thinking about something, then said:

"Do you remember the line at the very end of the story when Tinocchia and Pinocchio hold hands and start walking together?"

By now all the other six residents had left their tables and stood gathered in one tight circle about us. I looked at them. They were all enjoying this little scene. Suddenly, I felt a magical ambience, a tenderness, as if we were all one family, they, I, and through Violetta, even her father, Abramo.

"Yes, I think I do. It's a memorable line. When they are about to stroll toward the moonrise... 'Like two happy puppetti, we...'"

But Violetta cut in. "Ah, that's what I was waiting for... My father told it like this: 'Happy as a puppetta with her happy puppetto we...'"

"How do you remember that?"

"Easy." Again the old woman with the youthful personality looked around. I could see how happy she was to be the center of attention. "Because my father used to call me puppetta as a term of endearment."

"What an amazing meeting this is," I said warmly. "This is like out of a story book. It's almost as if destined... Did your father know Collodi?"

"Of course. Even though Collodi was much much older. He got to know the old man after he published *Pinocchio* and remained acquainted with him until Collodi's death in 1890. Collodi knew that my father liked to write."

"Did your father do any other writing?"

"Well, you see, starting as a young man, my father was the one who for decades wrote a new rhymed Purim-shpil every year for the annual synagogue Purim Carnivale."

"So, then, that marvelous, witty Purim-shpil in the book is his."

"What a question! As is the rest of the book. You see, the Purim-shpil was one of his tasks as cantor, in addition, of course, to creating new melodies for prayers. And it was Collodi who inspired my father Abramo to write a Jewish version of the Pinocchio story."

"Do you have a copy of your father's manuscript?"

"Alas, no. My father would narrate the story to me."

"In that case, once I transcribe it, I'll send a copy to you."

"That would be wonderful. Thank you so much."

"You know, I found it in the Siena Municipal Library. Do you have any idea how it got there?"

"I'm not sure. My father must have given a copy to Collodi to read. Then, in the tumult after Collodi's death, combined with my mother deciding to move to Venice, later, after my father died, for she had a sister here, we neglected to follow up on the whereabouts of my father's story. When Collodi died all his papers were likely given over to the Siena Municipal Library, where he wished his writings to be deposited. And whoever archived Collodi's papers did not distinguish between Collodi's work and anyone else's. That's the way I imagine it."

"Violetta, please forgive me for asking, but as a scholar I am obliged to inquire: Are you sure your father composed this work?"

"After all this, why do you ask?"

"Because on the very first page the author says that the manuscript was given to him by the beadle of the Siena synagogue."

Violetta laughed. "That's another one of my father's jokes. Like I said before, a purposeful distraction."

All this was too confusing. Who knows? Maybe Violetta was making all this up. At her age, who could tell? Perhaps the Pinocchio syndrome. But her nose did not budge.

I looked at the manager, hoping that while holding his face with his fingers would subtly move his index finger to his ear and make a slight, subtle circular motion with his finger indicating that – beware! – dementia had overcome Violetta.

But I saw no such sign. The manager was pleasantly following this drama with great interest.

I saved my best point for last. I wondered how Violetta could possibly squirm out of the next question I would ask:

"And what do you make of the author's dedication of the book to his friend, Abramo Livorno?"

Again the old woman laughed. The ninety-nine-year-old Violetta was really having a good time.

"Once more my father's humor. Aren't you your own best friend? You have to remember my father specialized in Purim-shpil comedy, with its fun and exaggeration. And he was also familiar with hoax literature."

"Oh, my goodness! It's amazing you use this word. This very same word, hoax, also ran through my mind."

"So you see, we think alike after all," said Violetta. "And I have one other proof, if proof is what you're looking for. Maybe you noticed it, or maybe not. Maybe because it was mentioned only one time, it slipped by you. Do you remember, at one point in the story, Geppetto is scolding Pinocchio for not telling Tinocchia his real name when he first meets her. Then, when Pinocchio speaks, he says sort of off-handedly, as if it were some kind of outlandish name, Pinocchio tells Geppetto, 'I didn't tell her my name is Abramo.' This is a little hint my father inserts into the text to show his connection with this work. Another example of Abramo Livorno's sense of fun.

"And so I tell you, my dear young man, *Tinocchia* is not anonymous at all. Even though it does not have an obvious by-line, the Tinocchia story was written by my father, Abramo Livorno, the *hazzan* for nearly half a century of the famous Siena synagogue. Perhaps my father never even thought of putting his name on this book, just as didn't put his name on the dozens of annual Purim-shpils that he wrote for the synagogue."

"And what a delightful, inventive Purim-shpil he put into this manuscript!"

Violetta smiled. "I know. And because of my father's friendship with the older Collodi, and because of the similarity of the title to Collodi's famous book, and because Pinocchio appears in it, the manuscript was mistakenly put into a Collodi/Lorenzini box. I'm sure you know that Collodi was only a pen-name, and that his real name was Lorenzini... There!"

And here Violetta nodded with a proud little pressed-lip smile. "Now you have it. The mystery is solved."

At this she took both my hands and said:

"Come, let me embrace you. I thank you for discovering my beloved father's story, which I only heard from him, chapter by chapter, when I was a little girl but never read."

And she put her arms around me and drew me near and pressed her cheek to mine, as if she were my mother and I her son.

Then I told her:

"As I said, Signora Livorno..."

"No no, call me Violetta, *per favore*."

"Thank you, Violetta. Soon as I return home to New York and have your father's manuscript transcribed I will send you a copy. And if this story gets published, you will get eighty per cent of the proceeds, and I will keep for myself twenty percent as translator."

"No no no. Not at all. I need nothing. I have no children. Just give a nice donation to this Old Age Home."

"You read my mind, Violetta. That is just what I was planning to do. I hope someone will publish your father's wonderful book."

And then a little twinkle lit up Violetta's still bright brown eyes.

"Come." She stretched out her right hand to me. "Shall we step outside and watch the full moon rising over the Grand Canal, Nipocchio?"

Curt Leviant has authored nine critically acclaimed works of fiction. He has won the Edward Lewis Wallant Award and writing fellowships from the National Endowment for the Arts, the Rockefeller Foundation, the Jerusalem Foundation, the Emily Harvey Foundation in Venice, and the New Jersey Arts Council. His work has been included in Best American Short Stories, Prize Stories: the O. Henry Awards, and other anthologies – and praised by two Nobel laureates: Saul Bellow and Elie Wiesel. With the publication of Leviant's novels into French, Italian, Spanish, Greek, Romanian and other languages – some of which have become international best sellers – reviewers have hailed his books as masterpieces and compared his imaginative fiction to that of Nabokov, Borges, Kafka, Italo Calvino, Vargas Llosa, Harold Pinter, and Tolstoy. The French version of *Diary of an Adulterous Woman* was singled out as one of the Twenty Best Books of the Year in France and among the seven best novels. *Kafka's Son* in the French translation was hailed on French television as a "work of genius" and by French critics as "a masterpiece."

But the most memorable praise has come from Chauncey Mabe, Book Editor of South Florida's *Sun-Sentinel*, who wrote: "Curt Leviant is one of the greatest novelists you've never heard of. His serio-comic novels, including *Diary of an Adulterous Woman* (the best novel I've read during the past ten years), should place him in company with Joseph Heller or even Saul Bellow..."